the hill

the hill

KAREN BASS

pajamapress

First published in the United States and Canada in 2016

Text copyright © 2016 Karen Bass
This edition copyright © 2016 Pajama Press Inc.
This is a first edition.

10 9 8 7 6 5 4 3 2 1

www.pajamapress.ca   info@pajamapress.ca

 Canada Council   Conseil des arts
for the Arts   du Canada
 ONTARIO ARTS COUNCIL
CONSEIL DES ARTS DE L'ONTARIO
an Ontario government agency
un organisme du gouvernement de l'Ontario
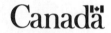 Canadä

The publisher gratefully acknowledges the support of the Canada Council for the Arts and the Ontario Arts Council for its publishing program. We acknowledge the financial support of the Government of Canada through the Canada Book Fund (CBF) for our publishing activities.

Library and Archives Canada Cataloguing in Publication

Bass, Karen, 1962-, author

    The hill / Karen Bass.

ISBN 978-1-77278-002-4 (paperback)

    I. Title.

PS8603.A795H54 2016   jC813'.6   C2015-907581-5

Publisher Cataloging-in-Publication Data (U.S.)

Names: Bass, Karen, 1962-, author.

Title: The hill / Karen Bass.

Description: Toronto, Ontario, Canada : Pajama Press, 2016. |Summary: "Seeking cell phone reception after a remote plane crash, young pilot Jared and local Kyle scale a hill that Kyle's Cree grandmother has forbidden him to climb. Coming down the next day, the boys find that the plane has disappeared, the forest has changed, and something is hunting them. A modern imagining of the Cree Wîhtiko legend"— Provided by publisher.

Identifiers: ISBN 978-1-77278-002-4 (pbk.)

Subjects: LCSH: Aircraft accidents – Juvenile fiction. | Airplane crash survival – Juvenile fiction. | Cree mythology– Juvenile fiction. | Values – Juvenile fiction. |BISAC: JUVENILE FICTION / Action & Adventure / Survival Stories.

Classification: LCC PZ7B377Hi |DDC [F] – dc23

Cover design: Rebecca Buchanan

Cover images: (front cover) © TTphoto/Shutterstock; (back cover) © BABAROGA/Shutterstock; (wolverine) © Jeane09/Shutterstock; (birch bark) © Tom Grundy/Shutterstock

Interior design and typesetting: Martin Gould / martingould.com

Manufactured by Friesens
Printed in Canada

Pajama Press Inc.
181 Carlaw Ave. Suite 207 Toronto, Ontario Canada, M4M 2S1

Distributed in Canada by UTP Distribution
5201 Dufferin Street Toronto, Ontario Canada, M3H 5T8

Distributed in the U.S. by Ingram Publisher Services
1 Ingram Blvd. La Vergne, TN 37086, USA

To Leigh.
For being a steadfast encourager.

Wake Up

The music throbbed through Jared's head, pounding a spike into his skull. *What the...I hate falling asleep with....* Eyes closed, he groped for the wires. Tugged so his earbuds popped free. The music stopped. The pounding didn't. Neither did the pain.

What's thumping? Turning his head drove the pain deeper. Something warm trickled down his cheek. Eyes screwed shut against battering hurt, he felt along his jaw, touched liquid warmth. Smelled his finger. Blood.

How...? Did I crack my head? Hangover? That couldn't be right. He'd stayed sober at the party. Hadn't wanted Mom's husband to hassle him. Confusion seemed to amplify the pain.

Why is it so hard to think? The pounding must be Mom trying to get him up and moving. He licked dry lips, couldn't get words out. He was already packed, ready for his mandatory three weeks with his dad in Purgatory, a.k.a. Yellowknife. Maybe he *should've* gotten drunk. Three weeks with no friends except the "buddy" his dad would assign to keep him amused and out of trouble. Real quality bonding time between father and son.

What time was it? The charter wasn't leaving until—

Wait. That wasn't right. His thoughts were spinning a story, but none of it felt real. A daydream.

Think, Jared. Make sense.

I'd—No, no way. His pulse hammered. He'd gotten on Dad's private jet. Had taken off.

Engines screaming. Voice loud and urgent. "Mayday!"

Jared vacuumed air. His eyes sprang open. He clutched the armrests and stared at the leather seat facing him. *We crashed? No way.*

Whatever had been thumping stopped, leaving only the insistent pulsing in his head. Vomit crept up his throat. He swallowed. Dread seemed to shrink his body, petrify it.

His frantic heartbeat buffeted his ribs. He squeezed his eyes shut and inhaled slowly—one, two, three, hold— exhaled slowly. *Thudthudthudthud.* Again. In, hold, out. *Thud, thudthud.* Again. His pulse slowed to something resembling normal. He was alive. Whatever had happened, he had survived. He wiggled his toes in his high-tops. Exhaled slowly. And he was in one piece.

Parts of that piece were aching, especially his back and calves. *The plane slewing side to side. Bucking. Pilot yelling, "Brace yourself!" Engines screaming. Thuds, cracks. Being pressed into the seat so hard it felt like he was breaking. Then nothing.*

Pulse jacked again, Jared repeated his breathing exercise. He knew he should move before he stiffened into a slab of hurting concrete. Keep moving, his swim coach always told them after a hard workout. Stay loose. But he couldn't convince himself to even turn his head, never mind get up. From the corner of his eye he saw that the front-facing seat across the aisle had collapsed forward. Between the seats, the door to the cramped washroom hung askew.

He managed to unbuckle. Then he clenched and unclenched his muscles, starting from the bottom. His feet were easy, but his calves seized up and started him gasping again. Finally the pain relented and he slumped into the soft leather.

Clank!

It's going to explode! Adrenaline jolted Jared to his feet. He swung toward the door to see it cracking open from the top, lowering with a hiss of hydraulics. Afternoon sunlight streamed into the cabin in an opaque curtain. Jared squinted, blocked the light with his splayed hand.

A silhouetted head rose into view, pushed by a torso and long legs. A rescuer. The head ducked as someone entered the jet. He braced his hand on the cockpit's wall. "You're alive? Me, I pounded on the window and you didn't move. Thought you were dead."

"No," croaked Jared. Was that the pounding he'd heard? Not his music, but this man?

The rescuer scanned the four-seater aircraft. "You the only passenger? How's the pilot?"

Blankness slackened Jared's features. He could almost make out the man's face. Jared stuttered, "I-I haven't-haven't checked." Didn't even think of the pilot. Crap.

The man swung over to the cockpit's open doorway beside him. Jared followed, hand braced against the closet that butted up against his seat. His head was thrumming. He shifted to lean on the wall by the door and tried to peer around the man. "Is he alive?"

"Yeah. Knocked out." The man straightened, turned. Jared blinked rapidly. The guy was as big as a man, maybe, but not much older than he was. He was huge, like some kind of real-life Hulk. The smell of wood smoke enveloped them. The strange teen's voice cut through Jared's haze. "You okay? You're looking pale...even for a white guy."

Jared leaned against the wall by the door. His mouth moved but nothing came out. Hulk stepped sideways and flung open the closet. Jared stammered, "W-what are you doing?"

"Need a first aid kit," he said, rifling through the contents of the small space. "Gotta stop the pilot's bleeding."

Who *was* this guy? "I'm bleeding."

He peered at Jared. "That's a scratch. The pilot, he's covered in blood." He returned to his search, pulled out a box with a triumphant look. "Help me get him out of his seat."

Jared tried to think. Everything seemed disconnected, like his brain wires had pulled loose. "Isn't it dangerous to move someone who's hurt? Shouldn't we be calling 9-1-1 or something?"

"Yeah, because the ambulance is just a few minutes away."

"It is?" Jared blinked in confusion and glanced at a window, but it was covered with a dirty smear.

Hulk gave him an unreadable look. "No. We're in the middle of the bush."

The pounding in Jared's head had flattened to an insistent buzz. And a white light seemed to be flashing just on the periphery of his vision, but when he turned his head the light moved too. "Where exactly?"

"Northern Alberta. Come help." He sidled into the cockpit and climbed into the co-pilot's space, propped a knee on the seat, and leaned over the unmoving pilot.

Jared's eye twitched as the mini strobe light brightened. It scattered his thoughts. "What are you doing?"

A quiet sigh. "Undoing his seatbelt." He leaned over the pilot, hoisted him up and toward the center console between the two pilot seats. "Come on. I can't do this alone."

He gritted his teeth, twisted, and pulled. The pilot's head, painted red like a garish mask, lolled and spattered blood on the floor and Hulk's coat. Nausea hit Jared at the same time as the blood's distinct coppery scent. He lurched to the open door, leaned on the wobbling handrail and vomited into murky water. His head began pounding again, and he stayed there a moment, gasping in musky air, before wiping his mouth with the back of his hand. He scowled at his hand, wondering what to wipe it on, then noticed his dangling earbuds. He tucked them into the pocket with his iPod. Something poked his neck; he slapped at it. Another pinprick; another swat. He retreated into the jet.

Hulk was still trying to get the unconscious pilot out of his seat. Jared tried to assemble his thoughts. "You're stronger than me. Why don't you haul him by the shoulders? I'll grab him around the waist when you get that far."

Hulk paused, then nodded at Jared. After several minutes of struggle, they wrangled the pilot out of the cramped cockpit and stretched him out on the floor. While Hulk bandaged his head, Jared slumped in the corner near the pilot's feet, careful to avoid any blood. Normally he'd resent some stranger taking charge and being so pushy. Right now, though, he could barely think, never mind argue. He rested against the bulkhead, head turned toward the cockpit as a memory surfaced of the pilot's strained voice. *Does anybody read?*

"I'm pretty sure the radio wasn't working when we went down. How will they know where we are?"

Hulk kept wrapping the pilot's head. "Me, I don't know. What happens in movies? Doesn't the blip disappear on some radar screen, then they send search teams?"

"That's the movies. Does it really happen?" Jared eyed Hulk skeptically.

He shrugged. "Don't pilots have to report where they're flying? Where were you going?"

"Yellowknife."

"Yeah? Lots of bush between here and Yellowknife, but a plane this fancy must have GPS and one of those black box things. It should be easy to find."

"I sup—" Jared's attention dropped to the bottom of the pilot's seat. "My backpack!"

It was wedged halfway under one corner of the chair seat. Jared strained but couldn't free it. Big hands joined his. Jared shrank away from the bloody fingers that grabbed the backpack's strap. One yank and Hulk freed it. Jared snatched the pack and unzipped it. He swore as he pulled out the dented laptop.

"It won't even open properly."

"At least you're not bent up like it is."

"It has state-of-the-art video editing software. I was going to edit a friend's skateboarding video." He glanced up to see Hulk's slightly raised eyebrows and twisted lip. *What the hell is that look for?* Jared knew scorn when he saw it. His eye twitched again.

Hulk's exhale was audible. "Do you know his name?"

"My friend?" What a stupid question. Then Jared noticed his gaze had shifted down to the pilot. "Oh. Mackenzie maybe? I don't know. He said to call him Mac."

After trying to wake the man up by calling his name, jiggling his shoulder, Hulk sat back on his heels. "I don't know what to do. Nothing seems broken but he might be hurt inside." He rubbed the back of his neck. "Got any food? We could watch for searchers outside."

Relieved at the thought of escaping the blood and its clogging smell, and the coffin-like feel of the small interior, Jared rifled through his backpack. He found his phone, which seemed undamaged, a granola bar and a crushed bag of chips. He got his electric blue windbreaker from the closet between his seat and the cockpit, put it on, and stuffed the phone and food in its pockets.

Hulk found a blanket in the closet and draped it over the unconscious pilot then led the way outside, down the steps and into the marshy water. Jared stood one step above the water as Hulk waded to shore, three or four yards away.

Had he shrunk? Inside the jet Jared felt like he filled the space, like he fit. Outside, the sky stretched into forever, but seemed anchored by spruce trees ringing the marsh. He felt like an ant, small and balancing on a broken twig. Clusters of reeds poked out of the water. Grass crowded the shore to the left but gave way to gravel or sand where the guy now stood, hands on hips. He'd been right—this was the middle of the bush. *Nowhereville.* A shudder rippled across Jared's shoulders.

"Coming?" Hulk called.

Jared shook himself, considered his CR high-tops, the water, then the wing barely over a yard to his left. It was slightly crumpled, and jammed against a broken tree that leaned over dry ground.

He retreated to the top step, gripped the hydraulic arm that stretched from mid-doorway to the bottom of the steps (the top of the door when it was closed), stepped over, and positioned the edge of his heel on the step. He swung his other leg over and lunged toward the wing, almost slipping off the curved edge into the brackish water. Falling to his knees, he scrambled forward, then paused as the light in his eye flashed again and a ripple of wooziness passed over him. He straightened slowly, tightrope-walked the length of the wing, arms outstretched, though it was wide enough to walk normally. When he reached the tree, he crawled along the wing's tapering length until dry ground appeared below him.

Jared dropped to the ground and steadied himself when his headache surged. His rescuer sat beside an army-green knapsack, arms braced on upraised knees, watching him with a puzzled look. Hulk's jeans were wet up to his knees and his hiking boots were dark brown from being wet. Blood stained one thigh of his jeans and a patch of his camouflage jacket, but he didn't seem to notice.

Jared suppressed a shudder and sat on the other side of the pack, on a patch of gravel softened by weeds. Hulk's curled lip of disdain returned. "Expensive shoes, huh?"

"Yes. They're Creative Recreation, leather and suede." The name obviously meant nothing to him.

"With a pretty gold stripe." Hulk nodded toward the marsh. "That plane, I bet it was expensive too."

"Three and a half million is what the pilot..." Jared looked at the jet for the first time since sitting. Mostly intact on this side, but crumpled and dented. Windshield webbed with cracks. A piece of the other wing protruded from the marsh about ten yards behind the tail. A line of broken swamp spruce revealed the line of descent. The seriousness of the situation hit Jared with the impact of a belly flop from the high tower. Pain blossomed in his chest and he found it hard to breathe again. The jet blurred.

Snap. Snap. "Hey. Hey. You okay?" Fingers grabbed Jared's chin and turned his head. "Should've already asked, but tell me your name. I'm Kyle. Kyle Badger." Fingers patted Jared's cheek. "Kokum, she'd say you're going into shock, but you'll be fine. You helped me inside. Only barfed once." His eyes squinted with a smile. "Come on. What's your name?"

Jared licked his teeth. Took in the high brown cheekbones, black eyebrows a horizontal line over dark eyes. Straight nose. He focused on the eyes. Not Hulk. "Kyle?"

"Your name's Kyle, too? That's weird."

Jared gave his head a little shake. His headache flared and his thoughts shattered like a glass smashing on concrete. *What? Oh, name.* "Jared. Fredrickson." He glanced at the jet from the corner of his eye, unable to look at it straight on. "Wh-why were you close by? Do you ... live near here?"

"Yeah. My teepee's just on the other side of that hill."

The mini-laser flashed in his eye. Jared cocked his head. "Really?"

Kyle snorted. "I'm at Moose Camp with Kokum and Moshum, and my little brother, Sam. It's not far. I was with Sam so I sent him back to camp to report the crash. If there's a way, Kokum, she'll come here with her big red stallion to rescue us."

Except for his mouth, Kyle was motionless, attention on the downed jet. Jared, on the other hand, was finding it hard to sit still. Mosquitoes and who knows what else had decided he was a buffet. He swatted and fanned and slapped, then jumped to his feet. "I'm getting eaten alive. How can you stand it?"

"Wet year. Lots of mosquitoes. You get used to it." He stood and stretched and peered down at Jared with hawk-like intensity. "You're a treat. Fresh blood."

"You're sick." Jared punctuated the declaration with a slap to his neck. "How long will your brother and"—he waved his hand—"those others be?"

Kyle shrugged. "Sam, he was running, but it's a ways. They'll come as soon as they can."

"That's no answer." Jared waved more mosquitoes away. "We need to do something."

"We need to wait. Stay at the scene of the accident."

"I-I..." Accident. Jared licked dry lips, eyes drawn again to the jet. He'd been in an accident. More than that, a freaking plane crash. Dad's company jet was a mess. The pilot was, was...He searched Kyle's face as unease ripped at his seams, threatened to explode into panic. Dad was going to freak out. "I'm in trouble. Big...I'm..."

"You're fine. Just, shook up." Kyle slid a hand into one camouflage pocket and pulled out a gray cloth. He dribbled some water onto it from a canteen, then gave it to Jared. "Wipe that blood off your face."

A few swipes and Kyle said, "Looks better. It's not bleeding, but you've got one super-sized bruise. Were you knocked out? Got a headache?"

"Yes, actually." Jared pressed two fingers against the corner of his eye where that mini strobe light kept flashing.

Kyle reached into his knapsack and pulled out a red wallet stamped "First Aid." He handed Jared two pills and the canteen.

"You have Tylenol with you?"

A shrug. "I could brew up willow bark tea, but it works slower and tastes real bitter."

Jared gulped down the pills and handed the canteen back with a nod of thanks.

Kyle held the canteen and studied the jet. "That pilot, I hope he lives. He saved your life, you know. You should've seen it."

The jet captured Jared's attention again. Kyle continued in a quiet voice, "It dropped out of the sky like it was making a landing. Something was wrong. It swayed, wings wobbled. Bucked like a bronco." He frowned up at the sky. "I think the plane wanted to dive straight down. If the pilot hadn't fought so hard, you'd be dead."

Kyle pointed beyond the jet. "We were by the edge of the slough. Had to take cover when the wings started clipping trees. Before it hit, the plane, it stopped screaming, like the pilot shut it down. Then, *boom*, the earth shook. Must've skidded the length of two hockey rinks. I bet the pilot took it down in the slough because it has soft ground."

Hands in his pockets, Jared hunched his shoulders. He hadn't wanted that picture in his head. The weight was back on his chest. "Do you always talk so much?"

"No. I hoped it'd keep you from freaking out. Kokum says talking calm is good to do if someone's dazed. Big thing to go through when you're a kid."

"Kid? I'll be sixteen in September."

Kyle gave him an incredulous look. "Really? I'll be sixteen in October. You're pretty short."

"And I love being reminded of that." Jared's fingers wrapped around his cell phone. It felt like the only piece of normal in this crazy day. They fell into silence, both eyeing the small jet. A few minutes later Jared's headache started to fade. He rubbed his thumb over the face of the phone and struggled to organize his circling thoughts. He had survived a crash. Help was coming.

Was it? What if it wasn't? What if Kyle was wrong and the GPS wasn't working? What if no one was coming? He couldn't stay out here. He was an ant. This place would crush him. He had...he had to call for help. Call who? Call 9-1-1.

His thumb kept rubbing the face of his phone. He froze. *I have my phone. I can call.*

"Stupid," he said to himself. He pulled it out and turned it on, tapping its back while it powered up. No service. He held it up in the air. Turned around. Nothing.

"What are you doing?" Kyle asked.

"We can call for help. And there's a GPS in the phone."

"No towers."

"No sweat. It's a great phone. If we get out of this swamp..." Jared turned again, this time scanning the horizon. He pointed. "That hill. Highest around. It's perfect." He stuffed his phone back in his pocket as he started forward. A mantra thrummed through his mind: *I can call. I can get help. I can call for help.*

"Wait," Kyle said.

Jared didn't wait. Instead, he started to jog, slowing to a brisk march when his body complained. His head cleared as he walked. Moving felt so much better than staring at that jet. He couldn't think about what might have happened. The sooner he phoned and they got a fix on his location, the sooner he'd be whisked to somewhere semi-civilized. *The phone is the key. I can call for help.* He heard Kyle jogging behind him, glanced back to see him packing his knapsack and a rifle. Jared did a double take. Tried to walk faster.

A small rise gave way to a wooded crease in the landscape. Beyond that, a hill loomed over everything. It was dotted with rocky outcroppings and clumps of trees. The crest was bald. It seemed out of place, a mountain in the middle of nowhere. Jared started into the ravine. Kyle grabbed his arm and jerked him around.

"I said, wait." Kyle's eyes were dark thunderclouds. "You can't mean that hill." He pointed with the rifle.

"It's the highest in the area."

"No."

"Why not? It's perfect."

Kyle was shaking his head. "Kokum, she warns us every year that no Cree, no *person* ever walks on that hill. We're not going there."

"Who is this *Kokum* person?"

"Kokum means grandmother."

"Because your granny says you can't go, you don't? That's lame." Jared yanked his arm free. "Stay by the jet and wait. I'm going up the hill to get cell phone reception. And with a little luck, these rotten mosquitoes will stay with you."

"Come on. There's no reception down here or up there. Stay at the scene of the accident. Remember? You aren't thinking straight."

"I know what I'm doing. I can call. I can get help." Jared skidded down the mossy incline. By a cluster of bushes, he looked back. On the rise, Kyle dropped to one knee and planted the rifle butt on the ground, muzzle pointed skyward.

He leaned against the weapon, seeming to cling to it for support. Head bowed, Kyle's hunched posture seemed to radiate anguish.

A chill settled on Jared's skin. He shook himself, swatted at a squadron of mosquitoes encircling his face, and plunged toward the willows that lined the bottom of the ravine like a fence. He pushed branches aside, creating a gate. No fence was going to hold him back. One way or another he was getting out of these woods.

2

Climb

Obsessed by the thought of calling, and driven by mosquitoes and the desperate need to get out of this wild place, Jared hiked as fast as he could. Which wasn't very fast. The underbrush tried to trip him. Low branches forced him to duck and weave. He clambered over a fallen tree and pushed a branch out of the way, only to have it whip back and flick his ear.

He stopped and rubbed the spot. Swore when mosquitoes started dive-bombing him again. A flash of movement caught his eye. He ducked to look under spruce boughs and saw Kyle, crouched down, watching him.

"What do you want now?" he yelled. Kyle wasn't going to stop him. Nothing was going to stop him from getting up this hill.

"It's easier if you're on the trail."

Confusion washed over Jared. "What trail?"

"Game trail." Kyle patted the ground.

Jared fought his way through the tangle of grasses and weeds intertwined with fallen branches. He stepped on something squishy and tried not to think about it. When he got to Kyle, he bent over and braced his hands on his thighs. "This is crazy."

"Yeah. Let's go down."

"Not going up the hill. This undergrowth. These mosquitoes. It could drive a guy nuts." He straightened. "I thought you were going back."

Kyle scowled toward the hilltop. "Kokum will be mad at me for going up this hill."

It sounded like a "but" was coming, so Jared waited.

"But she'd be madder for letting some stupid American city kid go up it alone."

"I'm not American. I'm from Edmonton."

Kyle pulled his head back, looked doubtful. "How does a kid from Edmonton end up on a private jet?"

As if Edmontonians couldn't be rich. "My dad's a CEO with a diamond mine in the Territories." Jared heard his own smugness and shrugged. "He's divorced from Mom. I refuse to go up to see him unless he uses the company jet to get me. So he does."

That was met with silence. And a blank expression. Finally, Kyle scowled in the direction of the swamp. "Me, I'd say getting your way didn't work out this time."

Jared shivered. "Just...shut up about that? Let's go."

"When you see your phone's useless, we get back down. Double fast."

"You *are* scared."

Kyle grabbed Jared by his coat collar, looked like he wanted to punch him, but released him and exhaled slowly. "My people only give warnings when there's good reason."

"So what's the reason?"

Kyle shrugged and peered toward the hilltop. He waved at the trail for Jared to go.

"You lead," Jared said. "You're the trail spotter."

Kyle's expression went blank again. The storm clouds had returned to his eyes, but he looked away, lips pressed together, and shook his head slowly, as if talking himself out of something. Jared's mom did the same thing when she was pissed off. What did Kyle have to be pissed off about? He had to know he'd get them to the top faster.

Kyle started up the trail. It wound through the forest and around rocks. Jared worked hard to keep up. He was in shape, but his limbs didn't seem to want to obey him, as if his brain were still short-circuiting. At least the Tylenol had helped his headache.

They didn't speak. The only sounds were their footfalls, Jared's breathing, and the constant whine of mosquitoes punctuated by slaps. They might have been halfway up when a flash of gray dived at Kyle's head. He dropped into a crouch and whipped his rifle into his hands. Then the feathered bomber almost clipped Jared's nose. He yelped and jumped backward, caught his heel, windmilled his arms to regain balance, then held his arms up like a shield and tried to spot their attacker.

Kyle shouldered his rifle. A gray bird perched on a

branch above them, peered at them with beady eyes, then started squawking. Kyle planted his hands on his hips and scowled at the noisy bird. It swooped at Jared's head again and landed on another branch. He avoided it easily this time.

"What is it?" Jared brushed his shoulders, fearful that the bird might have dropped a load, but he hadn't felt a plop, small or large.

"Whiskey Jack." Kyle tilted his head, squinted. "I don't think he wants us to go up."

"That's why the crazy bird attacked us? Give me a break." Jared picked up a twig and flung it at the bird. It screeched, flapped its wings, and settled farther along the branch. Jared could have sworn he saw its eyes narrow in displeasure. Which was crazy. It was a bird. He stalked past Kyle. "Stay with your feathered friend, if you want. I'm going up."

"*Moniyaw*, you are asking for trouble," Kyle called after him.

With a sharp cry, the bird swooped over Jared's head. Minutes later Kyle powered past Jared and retook the lead. The bird continued to follow or fly ahead and wait. Every time Jared glanced its way, it screeched again, so he kept his attention on the ground where roots and rocks and clumps of undergrowth continually tried to trip him.

After what seemed like hours, Jared stopped to rest atop a rock. He almost felt like puking again, and his headache was returning. The crash must have really zapped his strength. He shouldn't be this tired.

The stupid Whiskey Jack was nowhere in sight. Nothing was, except trees and sky. He'd never been in such a quiet place. He was used to noise, human noise, machine noise, not this awful silence. He started, realizing Kyle hadn't stopped and wasn't in sight.

Jared scrambled to catch up. A stitch in his side edged into pain and he pressed a hand against it. He tried to inhale more deeply, and sucked a mosquito into his mouth. He hacked and coughed up the insect. *Disgusting place.*

Kyle had stopped in a patch of grass. He scowled as he looked around, tilted his head and listened. His frown deepened. He glanced back with an expression that was dark—not really angry, more brooding. A blur of gray exploded into the clearing. They both startled. The Whiskey Jack circled a tree and flapped overhead again. Jared's heartbeat thundered, and he swore under his breath.

Kyle looked like he wanted to say something, but he clamped his mouth shut and continued on. As Jared followed he powered up his iPod. Music encased him in a zone of relative unawareness as he trudged along, head down, Kyle's legs on the edge of his vision. Occasionally the legs would stop, and Jared would glance up to see Kyle with that same haunted expression, looking for something he apparently couldn't find. Was he lost? Was something worse than a stupid bird following them?

A cluster of songs had played when Jared bumped into Kyle's back. Kyle spun, his lips pressed in a tight line. His eyes narrowed when he saw the iPod wires.

Jared popped the buds out of his ears and stuffed them in his pockets. By touch, he powered down the iPod. "Did you say something?"

Kyle faced the setting sun. One hand skimmed over his head, gave his stubby ponytail a tug, then dropped to hang slack. His shoulders rose and fell, a question mark or shrug of exasperation. The Whiskey Jack soared past him and disappeared into the trees.

They were on the hilltop, above the tree line. Beside them at shoulder height, a smooth bare rock the size of an Olympic swimming pool capped the crest. Boulders clustered along the far side. Stunted trees encircled the crown, low enough down the hillside to allow a clear view in every direction. The surrounding hills, all lower, were shadowed blue, and looked like ocean swells. Kyle's attention remained on the horizon.

Clouds rose to meet the descending sun; rays shot through the gaps. "Is a storm coming?"

"Something's wrong."

Jared tensed as he eyed the tree line below them. He didn't see anything, relaxed, and told Kyle as much.

"How long did we climb?" Kyle didn't wait for a reply. "This is July. The sun doesn't set until ten thirty."

"So we were climbing longer than we thought." Even as Jared said it, he knew it was wrong. He would've seized up like some rusting science fiction robot a long time ago if they'd been climbing for six hours. It had been four o'clock when the jet had left Edmonton. They had crashed barely forty minutes into the flight. One-third of the way? Maybe a bit more. After they landed, his dad would have taken him out to supper, just like every visit. His stomach growled. He clambered up onto the flat rock and pointed into the valley. "The sun's hitting something shiny down there. It must be the jet."

Kyle joined him on the plateau. "Yeah. That's it. You can see mist rising off the slough. Try your phone."

Jared powered up his phone as he scanned the landscape. "Mist is forming in every valley. Is that normal?"

"It's been a wet year."

Jared held up his phone, turned slowly. Not one bar of service. He tried sending a text but the processing bar didn't advance. *Failed to send,* the text app declared. "This really is the middle of nowhere. No chance you have a phone, is there?"

A snort. Kyle dropped to sit cross-legged on the stone. "Nope."

Jared joined him on the warm ground. "No phone? How do you stand it?"

Kyle shrugged. "Kokum has a phone I borrow if I'm going out. No texting, though. She's strict." He continued to frown at the horizon as he slung off his pack and rotated his shoulders. "We won't get down before dark."

The sun carried more heat than Jared had felt all day. As it disappeared, the mist continued to rise. It swallowed the jet. "Do you have a flashlight?"

"Small one. But we should stay. Fog makes it easy to get turned around."

Somewhere in the trees, a bird cried—it sounded like that gray bird again. Goosebumps crawled across Jared's neck. He suppressed a shudder at the thought of spending the night on the hill. At least the jet had a door they could close. "You got us up here. Down should be easy. You're a skilled hunter-gatherer guy, right?" He nodded at the rifle on the rock, muzzle pointed at the disappearing sun.

"Do you ever listen?" Kyle rubbed his neck then gripped one knee. "Fog, it turns you around. In the city, you've got curbs and streets to keep you oriented. Out here?" He shook his head. "An older cousin, he took me driving in fog once, in a field of bales. I knew a river ran along one edge of the field. Couldn't figure where we were or if we were gonna go over the bank with the next turn."

Jared waited to see if Kyle would continue talking. He seemed to slip into storytelling mode, then quit when he realized what he was doing. "So you were scared."

Kyle's lip curled up and his assessing look almost made Jared want to squirm. "Sometimes scared is the smartest thing you can be."

Cold crept up Jared's spine. The sun turned the rising mist amber, then shot it through with streaks of rusty red that made Jared think of blood poisoning. Fog snaked around hilltop islands, swallowed them whole.

Kyle popped to his feet, startling Jared. He pointed west. "Go look for deadfall," he said, and headed in the other direction.

"For what?"

Kyle stopped and spun on one heel. "Deadfall. Like it sounds. Dead branches break off and fall onto the ground. They'll be drier than live wood. Easier to burn."

Jared had wanted to protest, but Kyle left too quickly. He squinted at his CR high-tops, doubled over and brushed some dust off the suede inserts. His lower back twinged. He straightened, rubbed it, and scanned the sky, wishing a rescue helicopter would appear, spotlight raking the hill. Surely his parents were looking, if only for the great PR: *Distraught diamond executive reunited with son who survived plane crash.* His dad could do distraught if cameras were around. Behind closed doors he'd do angry. *Wasting my time. Blah blah blah.*

Jared kicked at a rock. Pain jolted through his foot when it didn't budge. He shook his foot and trudged under the trees, ducking to avoid branches. Minutes later he had an armful of deadfall. Back on the crest, Kyle crouched beside the stone plateau where a small overhang of rock offered some shelter. He built a pyramid of sticks, small ones tucked inside larger pieces. Jared dumped his load beside a pile that was four times the amount of firewood he'd collected.

Kyle sat back on his heels. "Dry kindling, it burns like paper. Get more before it's too dark."

"Every muscle hurts. I need to rest." Jared sank onto a rounded, knee-high rock. "You go if you want."

Kyle slowly pushed to his feet, stood stiff and tall as he considered Jared, then stalked to the edge of the trees. Returned. Shoved his hands into the side pockets of his camouflage jacket. Glared with clenched jaw and curled lip.

The silence iced the air between them. Finally, Kyle spat to the side. "Me not being white doesn't make me your servant."

Jared's hands jerked up like a shield. "Whoa, dude. Where'd that come from? I only said I was too tired to move."

"Then you ordered me to. Like I'm here to fetch water and carry wood. And spot trails." Kyle jabbed his finger in Jared's direction. "Your stupidity brought us here, so do your share."

"I. Can't. Move."

Kyle capped both hands on his head with interlocked fingers. He inhaled audibly and released a long slow breath. "Then we'll do without. My coat's warm. That fancy shell you're wearing, it won't keep you warm long. You can freeze your shrimpy little butt off for all I care." He retreated under the overhang, becoming a shadow in the growing darkness.

"Aren't you going to start the fire?"

"When it gets cold."

Jared crossed his arms, refusing to admit that with the sun gone he was already starting to feel chilled. The sky darkened to indigo, turning everything to silhouettes. Night was falling faster than he remembered summer nights doing in Yellowknife. Twilight lingered forever there. It even seemed to be getting dark faster than summer nights in Edmonton. Like Kyle said: it was weird. Jared scratched at a mosquito bite and realized he hadn't been bitten since partway up the hill. Only good thing about the whole crappy day.

Darkness thickened, and seemed to become infinite space around him. No walls, no limits. Could gravity be trusted in this nothingness? Jared edged toward the overhang and knelt beside it, then leaned against a rock, finding comfort in its solidity and waning warmth. "It's too big out here." He spoke mostly to interrupt the silence.

A quiet snort responded from the darkness. "You'd rather be in a mall, I guess."

"Any day. It has walls and a ceiling. Noise. People." He licked his lips wistfully, then powered up his phone and frowned at the backlit screen with its picture of him and his friends at the waterpark. Still no service.

"Wonder how the pilot is." Kyle's voice was a whisper.

"You did what you could."

"Was it enough? Pilots...Here in the bush and farther north, pilots bring supplies, get you to the doctor. They're your lifeline."

Jared heard what wasn't said. Pilots were worth saving. More important than rich city kids. "Then you should've gone back to the jet."

"Maybe. But you'd be up here alone. In the dark. No way to make a fire." A pause, and Kyle repeated, "Alone."

"Shut up."

"Sure. Get out that food you brought and I'll light the fire."

Kyle's flashlight almost blinded Jared. He kept it on long enough to start the fire with a lighter. They shared Jared's crushed chips, his granola bar, and water from Kyle's canteen. The fire crackled, hypnotizing Jared with flares of yellow as it devoured the wood like a ravenous dragon. Kyle suggested they sleep. He kicked dirt on the embers and made space for Jared in his stone-roofed shelter. Under the overhang of rock it felt like crouching in a foyer with a low ceiling. Jared imagined a cave at their backs, its entrance hidden. Something's lair. Though the fire had warmed him up, he shivered.

He had never been camping. Had never wanted to. And this was worse than anything he'd imagined. No sleeping bag or mattress, no tent. No friends to share the ordeal. Beside him, Kyle's breathing relaxed. Finally, earbuds in place, music lulled Jared to sleep.

He woke with a start. Something—

A screech made Jared cringe. He bumped his head on rock. "What the?"

"Owl hunting," Kyle muttered. "Go to sleep."

Jared rubbed his head, groped for the earbud that now dangled on his chest and popped it back in place. Silence. He fiddled with the iPod but couldn't coax it to play. His shoulders tensed. *One thing. Can't I have just one normal thing in this hideous place?*

Without music as a shield, the hilltop's vastness pressed down on Jared again. The rock at his back had lost its daytime heat and now felt cold, unwelcoming, like it knew he didn't belong. He shivered as he rebooted the iPod. *Please work.* A song flared in his ears and his shoulders relaxed.

The song was layered with static that grew louder, then quieter. It had to be the earbuds, but they'd worked fine during the hike. He scanned the darkness as he tapped the buds and fiddled blindly with the wires, trying to figure out where the loose connection was.

A slivered moon highlighted gray tendrils of fog that reached out between tree silhouettes and receded into shadow. As if the trees breathed the wisps in and out. In and out. Like the static in his ears. His throat clogged up. It was in sync. The fog snaked forward, retreated a little, then slithered closer with each breath. Jared's mouth went dry. *What's going on? Am I hallucinating?* The static grew louder as the fog crept toward the overhang. A soundtrack. No, the sound of the fog breathing.

He yanked out the earbuds. *That thump on the head rattled my brain more than I thought.* The silence became a buzzing in his ears, the night a suffocating sheet of plastic that was transforming from black to gray. Hatred for the "Great Outdoors" flared. The fog continued its relentless advance. It blotted out the trees, shrank the sky.

The moonlight filtered through the rising mist. Jared bolted up, hitting his head again. Movement in the fog. Again. Tension vibrated through his limbs.

He tapped Kyle. "Wake up. There's something out there." He struggled to stay calm, but calm was a long-forgotten address.

Kyle muttered. Lifted his head and squinted. "Just fog. Go to sleep." He shifted, muttered again.

Jared kept staring, certain that he'd seen... *There!* To the right, a small bear? The fog swirled and eddied, reformed into... *What the—?* A man? That melted away too. Jared shook his head. *I am hallucinating. Can concussions do that? Fog is just low cloud. Go to sleep.*

Eventually, Jared dozed, but kept jerking awake, haunted by dreams of fog men and breathing static. When dawn arrived, he was shivering, his eyes ached, and his head throbbed. He kicked Kyle's foot to wake him. "Fog's leaving. Let's get back to the plane." Those reclining seats in the jet would be heaven to sleep in.

"Huh?" Kyle stretched and sat up. "You look like crap. Didn't you sleep?"

"With a rock for a pillow and ground like concrete for a bed? Hardly. Plus my headache came back. I might have a concussion." *And I spent half the night hallucinating.* "How did you sleep so well?"

He shrugged. "Me, I sleep on the floor a lot. This isn't so bad."

"Why do you sleep on the floor?"

"You try sharing a bed with a little brother who kick-boxes in his sleep."

Jared blinked. "You don't have your own room?"

Kyle gave him a look that said he was stupid. Jared realized he had been. Just because he had his own room didn't mean everyone did. He wanted to ask how small Kyle's house was but swallowed the question and eased out from under the stone overhang. He rubbed his arms vigorously, then massaged his neck as he eyed the retreating fog. It looked as harmless as whipped cream in the morning light. "Is it always so cold in the mornings?"

Kyle joined Jared and peered down at him. "Sometimes." His stomach rumbled; Jared's replied. He retrieved a paper bag from his knapsack and withdrew two fist-sized pieces of flat bread, and handed one to Jared. "Bannock."

Jared sniffed it, then nibbled the edge. Dry but tasty. There were lumps in it, raisins and something else, blueberries maybe. "Why didn't we have these last night?"

"We would've eaten them and our stomachs would still be growling this morning."

Jared wolfed down his bannock. "Got anything else in that pack?"

"Later." He handed Jared the water canteen and two pills for his headache. "Drink."

"I'm still hungry." He glanced at Kyle's half-eaten bannock and licked his lips.

Kyle ignored the hint and clipped the canteen onto the O-ring of the shoulder strap on his pack, which was more of a messenger bag. He shouldered the bag and rifle, then scanned the hilltop with an uncertain expression. "Let's head down." He took a bite of his bannock and started off.

Jared glared at that broad back and thrust out his upturned hands in frustration. *I spoke, jerkface. Don't ignore me.* He injected sarcasm into his tone. "How do you know we're going the right direction?

"I notched trees on the way up."

"With a knife?

From somewhere under his coat, Kyle produced a knife and held it up. The curved blade was wider than a pocket-knife, and longer. Jared asked, "What kind of knife is that?"

"Skinner."

"For...?"

Kyle stopped and turned toward Jared. His mouth twisted again. "Like it sounds. For skinning animals. After you kill them."

The image of the knife red with blood drained the warmth from Jared's face, leaving him cold and parchment dry. He tried to swallow. "Kill?"

"Welcome to the bush. We kill things, then we eat them." Kyle lifted his jacket and slid the knife into a sheath on his belt.

The trek downhill was made in silence. The fog seemed to retreat before them with unusual speed. A few times,

Kyle stopped and squinted back up the hill, his expression a mix of worried and puzzled. He never explained why and Jared didn't ask. He was just glad to be heading back to the one piece of civilization in this place, even if it was a broken piece. When they reached the ravine at the bottom of the hill, Jared's heart began to rap a joyful beat. He grinned at the insanity of being glad to be back at a crash site.

Both of them charged up the rise, their toes kicking up puffs of dust. They ran headlong down the other side, and raced along the edge of the swamp. Kyle grabbed Jared's arm, hauled him to a stop, and pointed.

A patch of thin mist hung over the swamp's center. But there was no jet. It was gone.

3

The Jet

Jared gaped at the swamp. As the last whiff of mist evaporated, sunlight shimmied white among reeds and tree stumps and algae patches. A dragonfly whirred past, startling him.

The yawning emptiness of the swamp settled like a basketball of ice in his stomach and spread numbness to his limbs, through his mind. He couldn't think, could only stare at the shimmer. The light should have glinted off metal, not dirty water. The silence, interrupted only by the hum of a few insects, chipped at the ice, returned feeling to his extremities and allowed him to turn.

Kyle, too, stared at the swamp with gaping disbelief, his face tinted gray brown. He was so still Jared couldn't tell if he was breathing. Jared's gut started to burn. Between breaths, the ice had flashed into a fireball that expanded and overflowed.

"Where's the jet?" Jared yelled. "Where's the freaking jet?"

Kyle tilted his head toward Jared, who clenched his fists. "Notched the trees, you said. The only thing notched is your brain. You led us down the wrong side of that freaking hill, didn't you? Didn't you!" He shoved Kyle sideways, making him stagger one step.

Jared paced a yard from the shore, kicking puffs of dust toward the water, spun and paced back. Rescuers had probably reached the jet. Maybe his dad was even with them. And here they were, on the wrong side of the hill. His dad would be furious he wasn't at the jet—anything that took him away from work a second longer than necessary pissed him off.

Kyle still stood unmoving on the shore, hands jammed in his pockets, a frown of confusion curving his eyebrows into a black slash. Fists opening and closing, Jared ceased pacing and glared at him. This was his fault. Mr. *I-Notched-The-Trees.* Mr. *Welcome-To-The-Bush.* Like he knew his way around it. He couldn't even lead them down a hill without getting lost.

Kyle glanced toward him, and his puzzled frown deepened. He strode to Jared and extended his hand. "Don't worry, little dude. We'll figure this out."

Little freaking what? Jared could almost feel blood frothing through his veins. He knocked the hand away. "I'm not worried. I'm *pissed.* This is *your* fault."

"Hey, I wasn't the one who insisted on going up the hill."

"We would've been fine if you'd actually marked our trail."

Kyle's mouth tightened. "I did."

Flame surged through Jared, blurred his vision. "Don't lie to me!" He spewed venom in a spray of incomprehensible screaming, and kicked dust at Kyle. He never saw the hand. It came out of nowhere and hammered his shoulder.

Jared tumbled, scraped across dusty grass. Flopped onto his back. The world spun for a few seconds before returning to normal. The anger was replaced by puzzlement. He sat up, brushed at the dirt clinging to his jeans and coating his shoes. A hand appeared in his peripheral vision and he swatted at it.

Reason #1 why we could never, ever, *be friends in the real world: Really big guys always use their size to push little guys around.*

"Stay away from me."

"I'm sorry, okay?" Kyle crouched nearby, eyebrows furrowed. "Kokum always tells me to mind my size, to not hurt people. But you were going crazy."

"This whole thing is crazy," Jared whispered. He kept his attention on his jeans as he continued to brush off dust. He discovered a grass stain on one knee and rubbed at it. "Craptastic. Now look."

"It'll wash out."

"Don't be an idiot. These are raw jeans." Kyle's reply was a puzzled look. Jared's words were stilted. "It means I don't wash them. Ever. Don't you know anything?" Kyle's expression transformed to mild disgust. *Clueless jerk.* Jared scanned the clear sky as he recalled shopping with Elise, the French exchange student who was almost his girlfriend. Only an inch taller, she'd gushed over how good the jeans had looked on him. They'd sat in a corner booth at the coffee shop, knees touching, and they'd sipped mochaccinos while a tailor shortened his new jeans. "They cost two hundred dollars with tailoring." Two-ten with the coffees.

Kyle's forehead crinkled as he eyed the raw jeans. "What? Are they sewn with gold thread?"

"Screw you," Jared replied, but the heat of anger was gone, replaced with longing. Why couldn't he be back in the city, shopping with Elise. He scowled as he swiped at the dust-rimmed grass stain.

Reason #2 we could never be friends: he doesn't know what dressing good looks like.

Kyle shrugged and squinted at the swamp. "I did notch the trees. I saw the marks."

"You're trying to tell me this is the right place?"

"Yes." Kyle stood. "But it's different."

"I noticed." Jared slapped at the dust on his shoes. "The jet isn't here."

"It's more than that."

Jared exhaled with exaggerated slowness. He stood and shoved his hands in the pockets of his windbreaker. "Really? Amaze me with your brilliance."

Kyle glared at him for a full minute, then pointed at the swamp with a sweeping gesture. "It's smaller, like it would be in a dry year. Remember the mosquitoes? Hardly any here now. They were swarming when we left the jet. You complained about them, remember? I've only been bitten once since we got to the shore. And why isn't the ground spongy anymore?" He nodded at Jared's skinny jeans. "It wasn't dusty yesterday. And smell."

Jared sniffed. And again. "I just smell smoke from your jacket."

Kyle paced six steps away. "Smell again."

With a roll of his eyes, Jared complied. "It still smells smoky."

"Yeah. There's a forest fire somewhere. Might be a ways off, but we're downwind of it."

Both of them returned to staring at the swamp. Finally Jared spoke. "You can't think this is the same swamp the jet crashed into. That's impossible."

"I'd rather think you're right and we came down the wrong side of the hill."

"But you don't."

"No."

Jared shivered. "We should check. I mean, what if the rescuers are at the site, but on that other side? And, like a couple of idiots, we're staring at the wrong swamp?" That's what's happening. *Why is he trying to freak me out?*

Kyle's shoulders drooped and he shifted the rifle. "Yeah. Back up the hill." He kicked a rock into the water. "Dammit! That hill. Kokum said to stay away from it." He paced away from the water and back toward it, fury in his jerky movements. He dropped into a crouch, eyes scrunched closed, jaw clenched, lips moving as if talking to himself. Or praying.

Uncertain, Jared hung back, out of reach. "Come on, Kyle. Bad enough I flipped out. You can't, okay? Because there's no way I could knock you flat."

Kyle snorted. A laugh, maybe. "You don't like that much, do you?"

"What? I'm used to being the short one, but no, I don't like it."

"Not that." Kyle stood and looked down at Jared. "You. Having to depend on someone like me. A—what did you call me? A *trail spotter*? What is that, anyway? Someone who lives in the country? The trusty scout in a cowboy movie? Or did you call me that because you don't dare call me an Indian?"

The low morning sun threw Kyle's shadow across Jared, making him swallow. "I-I didn't mean anything by it."

"Sure you did." One corner of Kyle's mouth lifted. "Lucky for you, one rule of being in the bush is that you help if someone needs it. Period."

Jared liked that rule, because the alternative of being alone out here was enough to freak him out again. He hated being alone. A memory sideswiped him, of being three or four and visiting a zoo with his parents. He'd run off when they were talking with someone, then realized he was alone in a forest of strange adults' legs. He'd zigzagged all over, frantic, crying and calling for his mom and dad. Jared blinked the memory away. If only he could get found by a security guard again and returned to safety, orange lollipop tucked in his cheek.

Kyle tapped him on the shoulder. "Wherever you were, it's not getting us back up that hill. Let's go."

"Sure." Orange sweetness lingered in Jared's thoughts. "Can I have a drink of water first?" They each took a long swallow. As Kyle was clipping the canteen in place, Jared asked, "Where do we get water when this is gone? That swamp water can't be safe."

"There's a spring over by our camp—" Kyle frowned to the east. "If it's there."

"Yeah, right. The camp or the spring?"

"Either." Kyle marched off, leaving Jared to follow.

He's crazy. I'm stuck in Nowhereville with a crazy guy. As Jared turned, a white shadow flicked in the corner of his eye. A jet-shaped shadow.

He froze. Fear clawed his throat, closed it off. *Breathe, come on, breathe.* The shape, more like a translucent model, rested in the water like the real one had. He peered sideways, afraid to move. The sky swirled with gray mist. The spruce trees stood shoulder to shoulder, a black line of ominous sentries. They leaned toward him, rattled their branches in warning.

Jared gasped, spun back. The swamp was empty, the sky blue. His heart drummed in his ears. *What the—? That brain rattling I got yesterday is making me hallucinate again.* He turned away again, peering to the side intently. Nothing. He'd imagined it.

The jet. *Get real, idiot.* Unless he'd seen a ghost of the jet. But that made no sense. A *thing* couldn't be a ghost. Ghosts were always people or animals. Maybe it was like that old movie, *The Others,* that Mom's husband had let him watch when he was twelve. It had freaked him out.

"Maybe *we're* the ghosts and don't know it," he whispered. That was stupid too. That concussion was feeding him crazy thoughts.

He looked around. Kyle was topping the small rise edging the ravine at the base of the hill. He disappeared without looking back. *Alone.* Jared's lungs clamped shut. He started to run, the tightness in his chest aching. He pressed his fist to his breastbone as he ran. The pressure eased as he topped the rise.

Again he glanced back, caught a flash of white shadow. He squinted at the swamp but saw nothing. Real? Not real? A ghost jet? *No. No way. Freaking concussion.*

The clamp started tightening around his chest again. He licked suddenly dry lips. Without Kyle he didn't even have a water canteen. Jared plunged into the ravine. "Kyle! Wait for me!"

4

Shadows

They returned to the hilltop at a pace that fired sharp pangs through Jared's legs. As a swimmer, he was in good shape, but his legs were used to scissoring, not pushing his weight upward, and each step quivered through his calves. He lagged behind, barely keeping Kyle in sight.

As he trudged upward, he muttered, "Oh look, a normal green tree pointing at a normal blue sky." Farther along: "Another normal-looking tree. And what's that? A rock. Not transparent." He patted it as he passed. "Solid as...a rock. You watch too many freaky movies, you gullible moron." He wiped sweat from the back of his neck. "Do ghosts sweat? No, they do not." All the way up the hill he looked for opportunities to point out his own idiocy. No doubt about it: he'd been hallucinating by the swamp.

When they reached the plateau, Jared crumpled onto

a rock and huffed in oxygen. He watched with disbelief as Kyle bounded the length of the flat stone hilltop and back, then planted his fists on his hips and glared down the way they'd come. He looked ready to hit something. He turned his glare onto Jared.

Fighting the desire to flee, Jared lurched up onto the stone cap and joined Kyle. "So? Which way to the crash site?"

Kyle pointed at the empty swamp.

"Don't screw with me." Jared squinted, but there was no sign of a ghost jet. Relief plucked at the corners of his mouth.

"What are you smiling for? That's the only swamp in sight. You're the one who screwed us, leading us up this hill in the first place."

"Right. The oh-so-dangerous hill your cuckoo said not to climb."

Kyle seized Jared by the collar and hauled him close. His jaw muscles bulged and his nostrils flared. Jared's collar squeezed his neck. Kyle's lips retracted to reveal clenched teeth. One word slid past the barrier. "Kokum."

"Got it." Jared could only whisper. "You're big, tough, and could beat the crap out of me." His mind flashed back to a pool party two years ago, some stupid thing his dad had dragged him to because the client had a son a year older. A much bigger bully of a son. Half a dozen times the kid had tossed him into the pool. Both fathers had laughed, but his dad's eyes had held a warning to not make a fuss, that these people were important. More important than a soaked and miserable son. Jared grabbed Kyle's wrist. "Being bigger doesn't make you better than me."

Kyle pushed him away, rubbed the back of his neck. "And being rich doesn't make you better than me. Not here. You're on my turf, *Moniyaw*." He crossed his arms and returned his attention to the swamp he'd pointed at.

He'd used that word before. *What does it mean?* He hadn't said it with any venom, more like a nickname.

Jared stared at Kyle's back for a moment, at the way his body seemed clenched, then decided it wasn't worth asking. Kyle probably wanted him to ask, so he could show off or something. He marched the perimeter of the pitch-sized cap of rock, clinging to the hope they'd gone down the wrong side of the hill this morning. At the far end he caught a whiff of something rank, almost like the school bathroom when some joker made all the toilets overflow. He finished the circuit having spotted only a few glints in valleys that might have been streams.

Kyle hadn't moved. Jared rubbed his thighs. "We must be missing something. Maybe we need to go to the bottom of the hill and walk around its base."

"We saw the jet in *that swamp* last night."

"And it got airlifted out during the night by a giant helicopter that we never heard?"

"You could hope so."

"Hope that we've been abandoned in the middle of nowhere?"

"I can find my way home."

"Like you found the right swamp?" Jared nudged Kyle's elbow. "Come on. We need to search around the hill's base."

"First I want to check the camp."

"Your camp? I suppose it wouldn't hurt. If your grand-parents are there we can eat. And find out what happened to the jet. There's got to be a reason we missed it."

"Yeah, but say anything else about Kokum and I'll leave you to rot." Kyle spun and stalked toward the far end of the rock hilltop.

Touchy. Jared didn't care if his friends made fun of his parents, or grandparents. He'd even done it.

Reason #3 on the never-ever friends list: the guy is freaky protective of his family. He scrambled to keep up. "Where are you going?"

"Cutting southeast."

"How do you know that's southeast? How do *I* know you won't get us lost?"

Kyle stopped so abruptly that Jared almost plowed into him. He pulled something from his knapsack's side pocket and tossed it to Jared. A compass.

"Okaaay." Jared held it out. "I don't know how to use this."

"Weren't you in Boy Scouts or anything?"

"Hell no. Lame bunch of losers." Kyle wouldn't take the compass from Jared's outstretched hand so he tucked it into the same pocket as his phone, pulled that out and powered it up.

While Jared held up the phone, searching for a signal, Kyle kneaded his neck. His features shuttered. "Lame is depending on a cellphone, especially out here."

Jared tightened his grip on the phone, imagined it hitting that broad forehead. Instead, he shoved it back in his pocket and retrieved the compass. "Fine. Show me."

Kyle stared.

As he continued to stare, eyes narrowing to slits, Jared recalled their conversation from last night, the one where Kyle had felt like a servant. He cleared his throat. "*Please* show me."

The stoniness of Kyle's features softened a little. After a pause, he explained how the red arrow pointed to magnetic north, and how to adjust the compass housing to point to the desired direction, then how to get moving in that direction. After the lesson, they walked to the far end of the plateau. Jared fiddled with the compass then pointed to what he hoped was southeast. Kyle nodded. Jared felt absurdly proud as he pocketed the compass, like last year when his coach had praised him for finally conquering the butterfly stroke.

They clambered over a cluster of small and mid-sized boulders. Jared hopped off the last rock and was hit by a vile stench, similar to what had greeted him the time his stepdad had accidentally left a steak on the counter all weekend when they were out of town. "What's that stink? Dead animal?"

Kyle tilted his head. "Probably, but dead animals get cleaned up pretty fast in the bush. They don't usually have time to get that rank."

The breeze seemed to pick up the smell and push it high into Jared's nose. He almost gagged. But Kyle appeared fascinated by the stench. He followed it, chin raised, letting the smell draw him to its source. He stopped a few meters away and beckoned Jared, who followed reluctantly.

Kyle pointed at the mouth of a cave, an opening the size of a small basement window. Jared pinched his nose and bent over to peer inside. It was more of a tunnel, though he couldn't tell how far into the hilltop it burrowed. He might fit into the opening, but Kyle never would.

In a nasal voice Jared asked, "Something die in there?"

"That smell, it's rotten enough for that, but even in a cave, carrion eaters would find the meat."

Wind moaned out of the hole, carrying a fresh wave of rottenness. This time Jared did gag. He waved at the stink and stumbled away. Kyle joined him. A grunt-like noise burped out of the cave's mouth. Alertness rounded Kyle's eyes and one hand gripped his rifle's strap with white knuckles. His nostrils flared as he squinted at the cave.

Jared's mouth felt stuffed with cotton. He tried to whisper, "What?" but couldn't get the word out. What animal could fit in that hole? A bear? No. A wolf maybe. Goosebumps prickled over his skin and he shivered. Kyle turned toward him, worry naked on his face. They locked gazes for several seconds as Jared struggled to not freak out at the thought that the guy who liked the outdoors was freaked.

Kyle touched a finger to his lips and pointed southeast. Jared managed a small nod. He stayed in Kyle's shadow and glanced back every few minutes.

- ⸻ -

A few times Kyle halted for Jared to confirm they were still heading southeast. Among the trees the sun didn't help, but every compass reading showed that Kyle did know his way through the forest.

They reached the bottom of the hill and walked for another twenty minutes or so. Without warning, Kyle veered off the trail and ducked under some branches. Jared followed. Only his raised hand stopped a branch from whipping into his face. He snapped at Kyle to watch it; when he didn't get a reply, Jared backed off several steps to avoid boomeranging tree limbs. He caught up when Kyle crouched by a small pool of water, refilling the canteen.

Kyle handed it over and Jared guzzled water; it spilled down his chin and neck. He paused, swallowed more. He returned the canteen and wiped his mouth with the back of his hand. "Good water."

Kyle refilled the canteen, drank, refilled it again. "It's the spring we use for our camp." Furrows etched into his brow. Shadows almost hid his dark eyes.

"But that's good, right? We're saved. You're the hero. Why don't you look happy?"

Kyle pointed. "The trail, it doesn't look right. We have a cleared path from the spring to the camp. No branches slapping you in the face."

"You were doing that on purpose." Kyle's look was blank. Jared let it go and peered in the direction Kyle had pointed. Indents that could be animal tracks marked the soft ground by the water and became a trail even Jared could spot as it meandered around trees like a stream around rocks. "Maybe this isn't the right spring."

Kyle pushed to his feet. "Don't start that again. I'll show

you where we camp." He clipped the canteen back in place and ducked low to follow the winding path.

Jared picked his way along the trail, trying to avoid contact with plants but finding it impossible. He stepped over a rotting log, sank sideways, and braced his hand on a trunk. Yellow goo stuck to his fingers. As he tried to shake it off, his hand skimmed tall grass.

"Ouch! Something bit me."

Kyle returned to his side, held his wrist to look at his hand. Then he poked the grass with his toe. "See that plant with saw-toothed leaves, light green stringy flowers on top? Stinging nettle. Don't touch it."

"You could have mentioned that earlier."

"Me, I figured you knew something about plants. Nettles grow everywhere, probably even in the city."

"Not where I hang out."

"Yeah, I guess there's no nettles in malls."

"So I don't do outdoors, okay? *Please* tell me how to stop the burning." Jared rubbed the back of his hand. White bumps were appearing in a golf ball–sized red spot.

"Mud helps."

"Seriously?"

"It cools the stinging." Kyle used his finger to expose a bit of dirt along the path. He dribbled water into the depression, mixed it and scooped a blob of mud onto his finger. Black eyebrows arched in a question mark.

Jared crouched and scowled at the black oozing mess, but he extended his hand. Kyle dabbed on the mud, careful not to smear or press too hard. The cool moisture helped.

They both remained low, eyeing the mud plaster. Jared was relieved it worked, but inside irritation was equally stinging. *Why does he have to be right so often?*

Finally, he forced his annoyance aside and said, "I thought you'd want to get to your camp and see your, ah, Kokum. That's right, isn't it? Kokum?"

"Nothing's right today. Everything's different and..." Kyle wiped his muddy finger on his jeans. "Try not to bump your hand."

"You're scared." That earned Jared a dirty look. "Huh. Well you are. Point the way, then, and I'll lead." Jared started down the game trail, stung hand resting against his chest. When he tripped on a root, he lunged forward to regain his balance, then paused. Beside his knee, another stinging nettle waved from the breeze of his passage. He stomped on its stem near the ground. It snapped and swished away, into the underbrush.

A few steps later they reached the clearing. Behind him an intake of breath marked Kyle's silent passage, so different from Jared's snapping, cracking, stomping advance.

Jared paused at the clearing's edge. If this was a campsite, it hadn't been used in a long time. Grass and weeds choked the meadow. Trails snaked through it like veins in marble. Here and there patches of the greenery had been crushed or eaten. He was just about to announce that the clearing was empty when he saw it.

Her?

Not shimmery, not see-though, but pale gray. Foggy gray in a field of vibrant green. Another hallucination. *Where did this one come from? Why could I only see the jet from the side but I see this straight ahead?* He squeezed his eyes shut, opened them. She was still there.

A tall woman standing with jeans tucked into hiking boots, a camouflage jacket, long braids. And beside her, a fire also leeched of color. *My scrambled brain is seeing what it wants to see. Which is...what exactly?*

Rescue.

Kyle stepped beside him. "What are you stopping—" He inhaled like a person who'd been underwater too long.

Jared grabbed his arm. "Wait. You can see that? Or... like...what *do* you see?"

Kyle dropped his pack and rifle. "Kokum!" He raced toward the ghost.

"What? Wait!" Jared sprinted behind but didn't catch up until Kyle tripped and landed on one knee. Jared clamped onto Kyle's shoulder to slow his rise. "Dude, it can't be your Kokum. It's *gray*. And *see-through*. Like a, a freaking...ghost. Look."

"I am. It's Kokum."

She didn't look old enough to be a grandmother. Her hair, gray like everything about her, gave the impression it would be black if it weren't so shadowy. "What's wrong with her? And why can *you* see her?" *She's my mirage, not yours.*

Kyle blinked rapidly and seemed to see her for the first time. Really see her. He turned a shade of gray himself. He brushed Jared's hand away and advanced so they were only a few yards away. He called her. And again.

"Come on, Kyle. Stop faking. You're just trying to freak me out, aren't you?" *It's working.*

Fists clenched, Kyle dropped to his knees and screamed, "Kokum!"

The ghost woman had been staring straight ahead and moving her lips. Now her lips clamped together and her gaze searched the clearing, as if she'd heard Kyle but couldn't see him. He screamed again and her eyes widened. A frown curved her brow and she said something. A single word. Tilted her head and said it again. Jared guessed she was saying Kyle's name.

Wait. His hallucination could hear Kyle's scream?

The feeling of being caught in a dream wrapped around Jared like a damp blanket. Everything felt fuzzy, out of focus— even his thoughts. Nothing was making sense. Two movies had been spliced together, one color and one black and white. Only in a dream could two separate movies interact. *This can't be real.* Jared moved up behind Kyle, who was shaking. *He* thought it was real. "Help me out here, Kyle. I think she's saying your name. Is that really your grandmother?"

Kyle gave a slight nod, whole body straining toward the apparition.

Jared knelt in the grass. He wrapped his fingers in the long strands to anchor himself to reality. "So...you're seeing a middle-aged woman in camo and jeans and hiking boots? Braided hair?" Another nod. Jared rubbed his eyes, wished he could feel the headache from the crash. A concussion was better than a shared ghost sighting. Or whatever this was.

If possible, Kyle looked even paler. He was going to turn transparent soon. Insects buzzed. Somewhere a crow cawed. Jared cleared his throat, needing to hear a voice.

"Maybe we're still at the top of the hill, and it's night, and I'm dreaming."

"You're not dreaming. I'm not dreaming." Kyle's voice was scratchy, raw.

"That could explain why it seems like...she's here, and we're here, but..." Jared could barely believe what he was saying. "But not at the same time." He released a slow breath as he tried to make sense of this. "That's a dream zone, dude. Admit it."

"No," Kyle rasped. "It's the hill."

Jared clenched his jaw. Not again. How could a hill cause this weirdness? He yanked the grass entwined around his fingers. It sprang free of the dirt. He sniffed, eyed the grass roots. "What's that smell? Kind of sweet, almost like vanilla?"

"Sweetgrass," Kyle replied in a hoarse whisper. "She's burning sweetgrass and praying."

As if. First she could hear Kyle, now they could smell her fire? No. Just no. Jared dropped the grass. "O-kaay. What does that do?"

"It's..." Kyle doubled over, almost touching his forehead to the ground.

"Hey." Jared tapped his shoulder. "Stay with me, Kyle. You're the only one who might know what's going on here." The calmness in his voice amazed him. He felt anything but calm. He sat back, cupped his forehead with his hand, and searched the clearing for signs of normal. The grass seemed normal. The trees looked normal. The cloudless sky. Everything around them said they were in the freaking Great Outdoors, when they should be at the jet getting res-cued. Well, everything except that ghost woman they could apparently both see. His breathing grew shallow. This was too much. Bad enough he was in the middle of a forest, but to have to deal with plus-ten weirdness just...too. Much. "Talk to me, Kyle. This doesn't make sense. You said that this is your turf. I need your help. You know how useless I am out here. No street signs. No GPS. No cell service."

Jared blinked. *My phone.* He booted it up. Counted out thirty seconds until it was ready. "What are you doing?" Kyle cast him a puzzled look.

"Taking a picture." Jared touched the camera app. He showed Kyle the screen. "We can both see her, right?" He touched the red circle, heard the familiar click. They both stared at the screen. Moisture fled Jared's mouth again. The picture showed an empty meadow. He frowned at it, at the apparition, back at the camera.

Kyle groaned, rocked for a moment, then straightened. His cheeks looked damp. Focusing on his eerie grandmother, Kyle said, "Kokum is here. But only partly. How can that be?"

Jared nodded, thankful Kyle was thinking again. "Okay, how? I'm thinking dream is a good option."

"Dream? We're both dreaming the same dream?"

"No. You're in my dream." Jared squinted one eye. "Or I'm in your dream. No. That's too weird."

"Maybe she really is here and we are, too."

"Wouldn't she be in Technicolor then? Black and white is only normal for old movies."

"Yeah. But what if...?" His cheeks turned pasty again, like gray play dough. He closed his eyes and shook his head.

"Tell me what you're thinking, Kyle. We've already

blown the weirdness scale."

"Not by half, *Moniyaw.* Not if..."

"Spit it out."

"Okay. You asked for it." Kyle bit his lip, winced and drew a long, slow breath. "Maybe we're in the same place, but at different times."

"Time travel? That's crazy talk. Are you sure that sweetgrass stuff doesn't make you high?"

"It doesn't. You use it in prayer. She senses we're in trouble. That's why she's praying."

"This is insane. Let's pretend for a second that you're right. Then you need to know..." Jared swallowed a lump, as unease crawled up his spine like ants swarming out of a hill. "I saw something else."

Kyle snapped his attention to Jared. "What?"

"The...the jet. When we were leaving the swamp the second time and I was turning away, I saw something out of the corner of my eye. A gray ghost jet. But when I looked straight on it wasn't there."

Kyle pushed his shoulder. "Why didn't you tell me?"

"I thought I was hallucinating. Because of my head getting knocked. I was freaked." Jared pointed. "So if you're right, why can we both see her when I could only see the jet from the side?"

Kyle squeezed his eyes shut. "Maybe it's the sweetgrass. It's an offering. To good spirits. Asking them to help."

"Spirits?" Jared's stomach seemed to plummet three storeys. "So what is it? Do you think we time traveled? Or do you think we're dead?"

A brown hand struck with rattlesnake speed, pinched Jared's wrist. He yelled. Kyle poked him. "Does that feel like dead? We're *not* dead." He stared blankly for a few seconds, then dread rounded his eyes, angled his brows into a deep vee. "Not time travel. Not dead. But we might wish we were."

"Cut the drama." Jared's voice quavered. "So what do you think happened?" He couldn't help looking at Kyle's grandmother again. Clamminess crept over his skin.

"I don't want this to be right. But..." He squeezed his eyes shut for a second, exhaled slowly, then met Jared's gaze. "Maybe we didn't time travel. Me, I think we're...in the spirit world, and the sweetgrass is pulling back the curtain so we can see Kokum."

"You think we're, like, in another dimension? Right. That sounds *so* logical."

"It is logical. We're in the same place but not. How do you explain that? I think that walking up that hill—"

Jared leapt up. "*Don't* blame this on me! No way. *You* are crazy. If we're not dead then I'm dreaming. That's the only explanation. The jet crashed, I'm unconscious in the hospital, and you"—Jared stabbed his finger at Kyle—"you're part of this crazy dream."

He stalked away, slapped his own cheek and whispered, "Wake up, you moron." He kicked at a scrubby wild rose along the path they'd forged. Kicked and kicked at the base until it started to uproot. He grabbed it by the stem, yanked it from the ground and threw it toward the hill lurking to the northwest. A cry dragged from his throat and he glared at the half dozen thorns hooked into his palm, then plucked them out. He heard Kyle approaching.

"Get away from me, dream boy."

"I'm not a dream."

"Of course you are." Jared pinched the last thorn, pulled and flicked it away. "Because this sure as hell isn't happening."

Kyle spun him around. "I'm not part of a dream. I'm Kyle Badger. I'm *Néhiyawak,* Cree, with a Déné grandparent. And I saved your carcass."

"I dreamed the name. Dreamed you. I'm dreaming all of this."

Kyle pushed his shoulder. "You don't know a thing about me or my life. You with your mall rat friends and private jets, you've never met anyone like me, so how could you dream me?" He shoved again.

Jared staggered backward. "Stop it!"

"This is real." Another push.

This time, Jared pushed back, both hands striking Kyle's chest.

Kyle retreated a single step and offered a twisted grin. "Do I feel like a dream? Maybe you don't want to believe this, but you don't have a choice. It's happening."

"Shut up. Just shut up." Jared shouldered past the taller teen and marched toward the ghost woman, Kyle's kokum. His eyes burned and watered and he blinked rapidly to fight back unwelcome tears. He halted a dozen steps away from the wraith-like figure and willed himself to wake up.

Kyle joined him. "I don't blame you. Me, I should have punched your lights out and carried you back to that plane when you first headed for the hill. I knew it wasn't safe." He pointed at his grandmother. "She knows we're close. She feels us."

"Why are you so freaking ready to believe that spirit world crap?"

"It's happened before. A story my moshum told about an ancestor."

"What's a moshum?"

"My grandfather."

"So he told you a story about someone going into some spirit world, and you believed it? Maybe if you were six."

"Stories are how we've always passed information, how we've kept our history."

"History, huh?" Kyle's expression shuttered like a blind closing. Jared shrugged. "Aren't you going to tell me?"

"Storytelling is something to be respected. I can see what you think, so no, I'm not giving you my family's story." Kyle crossed his arms and faced his grandmother. Longing and fear flickered across his expression.

"Freaking insane," Jared whispered. "Why does this feel so real?"

Reason #4 we'll never be friends: he believes weirdness, and expects me to believe it. Despite Jared's attempt at mocking, Kyle's obvious contempt emptied Jared's lungs. He felt like he'd just swum a dozen lengths of the pool full out. His heart slammed wildly in its cage—trapped, like he was. Words breathed out, a barely audible plea. "Let it be a dream."

They both watched as Kyle's grandmother continued to pray. She scooped the air above the flames and lifted it

skyward. There was something calming in her graceful movements. Jared's pulse slowed. Her hand swooped over the
flames again, gathered invisible smoke and ushered it up to
whatever spirits she called upon.

Kyle yelled, "Kokum, help us!"

Jared startled. The grandmother's eyes widened as something like fear took over her expression. She started to yell
in eerie silence. Her mouth formed a single word, again and
again.

Jared peered intently. "I think she's saying—"

They looked at each other as clouds cast the glade into
shadow. In stereo, they whispered.

"Run."

5

Flight

Run. Jared squinted at the phantom woman silently screaming the warning to them.

With a shrug, he pivoted to survey the meadow. A bird flitted across the far end of the clearing. A robin-sized bird. Nothing that could harm them. It didn't even look inclined to crap on them. The powder blue sky paled to misty blue near the horizon but the single cloud skimming away didn't look threatening. The air still held a faint hint of wood smoke, no worse than this morning.

Out of habit, Jared checked for a signal on his cellphone. Not a blip of reception. As he powered it down, Kyle raced across the meadow to where he'd dropped his bag and rifle when he'd first noticed his grandmother, shouldered them, and raced back. He was scanning the area, too, but with a look that seemed to expect a herd of rampaging moose to thunder out of the forest at any second.

Kyle grabbed his arm. "Gotta run."

Jared yanked free. "I'm hungry." He brushed at his sleeve and strove to ignore the incredulous glare burning into his composure.

"You heard Kokum."

"No. I *saw* your ghost grandmother yelling at us. Silently. From another dimension, if your insane theory is right. The so-called danger is probably in her dimension. And I'm hungry. All we've eaten is that bread you doled out earlier. You said you have other food."

This time Kyle's grip was unshakeable as he began to pull Jared across the field. Kyle kept moving, dragging him as he tripped on a tangle of rosebush and grass. Something snagged Jared's coat and ripped. Something else caught his sneaker and almost tugged it off.

"Stop it, jerkface. Let me up." Jared hit Kyle's thigh with his free hand.

Kyle halted but didn't release his grip. Jared regained his feet and slid his heel back into his shoe. "Let go of me."

"Only if you promise to run. We'll eat when we stop."

"This is crazy."

Kyle didn't answer. They both turned to look back at Kyle's grandmother. The sunlight infused her misty figure with light, made it glow like an electric candle, not flickering, but steady and strong. The figure still yelled soundlessly. Unease clogged Jared's throat for a second and he shivered, though the morning promised a hot day.

"Fine." He squinted at the hill sulking in the west. The sunlight bathed the slopes, yet the hill itself seemed like a shadow. Or something hiding in the shadows. It might be covered in rocks and trees, but it was a black hole, absorbing light, sucking everything into it, trying to suck them in too. Jared shook his head. "Which way?"

"Not back there." Kyle nodded at the hill. "That place is the problem. Whatever is coming will come from there."

Trying to fling off the shadows clinging to him, Jared imitated the famous music from that old shark movie, *Jaws*. "Da-da, da-da, da-da." Kyle looked like he wanted to hit him, but instead he spun and jogged toward the trees. Carrying the food.

Jared's stomach growled. He couldn't remember having a dream where hunger gnawed his gut like this. He couldn't let his only food source disappear, so he followed Kyle, calling for him to slow down. But Kyle was taller with a longer stride, and he opened the gap between them, forcing Jared to speed up. "Fast food" took on a new meaning, one that Jared didn't appreciate. He sprinted after Kyle.

Under the trees, roots popped up to trip him, and dead limbs that stuck out like sharpened stakes tried to stab him. He wove and dodged, jumped over a log. The sunlight flashed between the branches, a kaleidoscope of browns and light and dark greens.

Then Kyle was gone. One moment he was there, ducking around a huge spruce tree, and the next he wasn't. No movement winked between trees. No backpack thumped in time to footfalls. There was only silence and the spicy sweet smell of evergreens. Jared's lungs seized as his pulse raced. Knee-deep in the uneven carpet of weeds he turned.

Turned again. He opened his mouth to yell to Kyle to quit joking around. The silence seemed to stuff a rag in his mouth.

His air expelled in huffs as he wondered if someone could disappear between one instant and the next. The silence rang in his ears.

He had this dream sometimes. *He is on the high-dive platform, toes curled over the edge, looking down at his teammates swimming lengths in the dedicated lanes to his left. All the parents on the bleachers focus their attention on him. He raises his hands, springs into the air, jackknifes, then snaps out of it to dive straight as a pencil. He's bulleting down headfirst when he sees the water disappear.* This felt like that but without the familiar pool, the splashes and echoed shouts. Just the terror of falling toward concrete. Falling, concrete racing up toward his face. Never hitting, but feeling like his chest would explode. This dread was green and brown and dappled with sunlight, too quiet, motionless. Empty. A vacuum venting his lungs, leaving him unable to breathe.

Twee-wee. Twee-wee. Jared spun in a half crouch. His pulse drummed in his ears. A brown hand waved from behind a moss-covered log. Relief unlocked Jared's knees and he almost fell. He stumbled to Kyle's hiding place and braced his hand on a skinny white trunk that looked like it was peeling. "You jerk. I thought you had disappeared or something."

"Camo." Kyle plucked his coat sleeve.

"But I saw you moving through the trees, then—*poof*—you were gone."

"I stopped moving. That's when camo works, when you aren't moving."

A frown curved Jared's brow and he picked at a flap of bark as the last tremors of panic retreated. A thin strip tore loose and curled like paper.

"Leave the birch alone. The bark, it's a gift to my people. We don't waste it."

Jared ran the bark strip between his thumb and index finger. Its smoothness was paper-like and he continued to pull it through the roller press of his fingers. "I thought we were supposed to be running."

"Get down."

Kyle had stretched out on a bed of moss punctured by the odd weed. Jared brushed his fingertips across the seam of his jeans, and glanced down at that annoying grass stain.

"Now." Kyle's scowl was fierce.

With a sigh, Jared lowered himself onto the surprisingly soft surface. "I'm getting tired of you bossing me around."

"My turf, you said. If I go to Edmonton, you can boss me."

"Like that will happen." Bugs crawled amongst the strands of shaggy moss. Jared started to draw back but Kyle clamped onto his arm.

"Don't move. Bad enough you're wearing bright blue."

"There are bugs."

"Beetles. They eat logs, not people."

"I don't like things crawling on me." A rich earthy smell enveloped Jared, reminding him of the red wood chips the gardener put in the flower beds. Jared brushed a bug off his hand. One crawled up Kyle's sleeve; he didn't seem to notice.

Reason #5: he likes hanging out in the Great Outdoors, *with bugs, and stinging nettle, and who knows what else.*

"Shh." Kyle peered over the log toward the barely visible clearing.

"Why are we here? Your grandmother said to run."

"Me, I want to see what we're running from."

Jared began to speak again, but an exasperated look from Kyle silenced him. He tried to figure out why he was listening to Kyle aside from their size difference, and settled on the place. It felt different. Nothing he could pinpoint, just a sense of being *elsewhere*. Glimpsing a jet shadow from the side, seeing the ghost grandmother, had added to the oddness. He clung to the dream theory, even though any time he'd dreamed about a strange place, it quickly got drug-trip weird, with suddenly changing rooms and shrinking people and flying like an airplane with arms outstretched.

Birdsong began somewhere behind them—cheerfulness that countered the tension radiating from Kyle, the sense that every nerve was on high alert. The chirping cut off with a flurry of wings.

Kyle rotated his head ninety degrees. His eyes darted in their sockets like pinballs as he studied the forest. His head swiveled in the other direction. Sweat gathered along the nape of his neck. The sight made Jared aware of his own musk, edging to sour.

Snaps and muffled beats sounded off to the right. Gained volume, intensity. Something was crashing through the forest. Toward them.

Dread squeezed Jared's chest. Kyle stretched his arm to the right and pulled his rifle close, rolled so his back was to Jared, who was forced to peer between ear and shoulder.

Kyle's arm jerked slightly, creating a noise that sounded familiar. Jared had seen enough movies to know Kyle had just readied his rifle. But he didn't raise it or take aim.

"What—?"

"Shh."

The snaps became cracks. Thuds vibrated in Jared's stomach. Brown blurs zigzagged. Closer.

"Duck." Kyle flattened himself.

Jared buried one cheek in moss, one eye wide. His heart matched the approaching racket. Brown and white flashed over them. Around them. Antlers. Eyes. Black hooves. Twigs showered onto them. Jared turned his head to watch brown butts with a splash of white disappear.

"Deer?" he whispered.

"Mulies." Kyle exhaled.

"I thought they were deer."

"Mule deer. We call them mulies. Never seen them panicked like that. Not in the bush."

"So it's over. Whatever it was." Jared started to rise.

Kyle yanked him back down. His head smacked the mossy log, its green and yellow padding saving him from injury. Jared opened his mouth to complain but Kyle's attention was focused on the meadow, neck craned to see what was happening. Jared hunkered against the log, one eye squinting above its trunk. He felt the uneasiness rolling off Kyle in waves, and wished he could be one of those beetles burrowing into the moss.

Something brownish whisked across the meadow, appearing in brief glimpses between trees, like stop-action photography. Blink. Blink. Blink. Something upright. Flapping.

Then nothing. It stopped out of sight, beyond a cluster of trees.

Kyle's voice was barely louder than breathing. "Kokum's motioning. Talking to it. If it's a spirit it will hear."

"Talking to what?" Jared matched his volume.

Kyle's lips pressed together for a few seconds. "She's distracting it. Giving us time." He eased into a crouch, shouldered the bag, and picked up the rifle. "Come on. No noise."

Jared rose, grabbed Kyle's wrist. "What is it?"

"Don't know."

Worry fanned out from Kyle's eyes and tightened his lips again. He was lying. Jared couldn't bring himself to push the point. He released Kyle's wrist. A wave of anxiety washed over him as Kyle snuck away without looking back. Following was his only choice.

He avoided touching trees, tried to watch where he was placing his sneakers with each step. But Kyle moved fast for someone not making noise. Jared sped up, cringed at each snip, each click of a broken twig.

Hoping to wake up from this dream, Jared pinched his own cheek. It stung, but that was all. A good fifteen minutes later they reached a stream. Kyle rubbed the back of his neck, making his stubby ponytail bob, and scowled as he looked back the way they'd come.

"Safe now?" Jared bent over, relieved to have the chance to catch his breath. They'd moved faster each minute, without ever breaking into a run. He wiped the remnants of a web off his sleeve and flapped his hand to rid it of the sticky threads. He squatted and swished his hand in the cold water.

"No," Kyle finally replied. "We woke it up, so it's looking for us."

"Woke what?" Jared straightened and flapped his hand some more to dry it.

There was that look again. Kyle knew *what*. He shook his head and squeezed his eyes shut. "I wish this was a dream, that it was all happening in your head."

"You're trying to scare me." Jared offered a weak smile to prove it wasn't working. It immediately faded. "I saw something that flapped. What was it?"

"I, I can't—Kokum was right. We have to run. Maybe there's help out there." He waved downstream. "Somewhere."

"Tell me what it was. You knew, back at the clearing."

A small shake of his head. Kyle seemed pained, like it was taking effort to even talk.

Afraid.

Pulse speeding up, Jared grabbed the front of Kyle's jacket. "I have to know."

"If I say, it might hear its name."

Jared tugged the jacket, refusing to let go. Kyle sighed, leaned down and whispered in Jared's ear, so quietly it was almost inaudible.

"*Wîhtiko.*"

6

Worth a Try

Jared had never heard of any *Wîhtiko*. "Sounds like someone with bad gas."

The look he got almost peeled off his skin. Jared shrugged and sat on a rock. "I'm tired, hungry. I can't keep going. A meaningless name isn't a reason to get even more lost than we are."

After another minute of skin-peeling glare, Kyle gave up to scan the area. Not far away some birds chirped. Kyle tilted his head toward the sound. Then he set down his things and crouched beside them. "You've really never heard of... you know?"

Jared shook his head.

"I shouldn't be surprised. It's a Cree legend. Why would the white city boy know anything? It's always hungry. And it craves human flesh. Some nations called it

73

Windigo." He barely whispered the last word. When Jared shook his head and didn't say anything, Kyle continued. "Lots of elders and parents use...it...like a bogeyman. 'Watch out or *it* will get you.' Some of our stories are about men or women who become *wîhtikos*—cannibals—and have to be destroyed. But I'm pretty sure that this, this is *the Wîhtiko.*" The last word was mouthed instead of spoken.

"A legend?" Doubt seeped into Jared's tone. "So we're running from something that doesn't exist."

"Who said legends don't exist? If I'm right and we've stepped into the spirit world, *Wîht*—It's as real as we are. Here."

Jared exhaled the silent desire to wake up. "Okay. How do you destroy it?"

"Kokum told us a story about Wesakechak, a Cree trickster, getting an ermine to crawl down its throat and kill it from the inside."

"I don't even know what an ermine looks like. Do you speak ermine?"

The question hung between them. Annoyance oozed across Kyle's features. "Sometimes it's like you have a deep well of stupid."

"Whatever. I'm trying to come up with an actual idea here." Jared fell silent, thoughts leap-frogging over each other. *I'm dreaming. I must have heard or read about* Wîhtiko *somewhere, a movie or comic maybe.* Windigo *sounds more familiar though. From a video game?* "Maybe this is like a game playing out in my dream. If we beat the monster, we win the game and get magically transported home. Or in my case, I wake up from my coma."

"Beat?"

"Sure. Why not? You said it's always hungry. So maybe all we have to do is feed it."

"Are you offering to sacrifice yourself?"

"Now who's being stupid? This is *my* dream, *my* game. I want to win. Always hungry, you said. So what if you used that rifle of yours to shoot something big enough to feed it? I don't know. A moose, maybe."

Kyle snorted. "This rifle's too small to bring down a moose."

"Moose baby then."

"A calf? The mom'd trample you just for coming near her baby, never mind shooting it."

"Something else then."

Kyle laid the rifle across his lap, the barrel pointing away from Jared. He stroked the wooden stock, flipped the bolt back and forth, his features folded in thought. Finally, he looked up. "This rifle, it could take down a small doe or a small bear. It'd have to be one shot, maybe a second if the animal goes down thrashing. The instant that first shot's fired, *it* will hear and will race straight to us." His eyes were shadowed black with worry. "Is that what you want? Really?"

"If it gets this *Wîhtiko* thing off our backs, the risk is worth it."

"I don't know. I'm not as sure as you are. Because whatever this is, it isn't a dream." Kyle propped the rifle back against the nearest tree. "When it arrives, what then? Why would it go for the carcass and not us?"

Jared hunched over his knees, muffling the growl of his stomach. "Could we trick it into thinking the animal was a person?" He fingered the rip on his jacket from when he'd fallen in the meadow. "You were right. This coat doesn't keep me warm, but it does look very...manmade. We could prop up whatever you shoot and drape the coat over it. That might fool your monster if it isn't too smart."

Kyle stood. "It might work." He donned his pack and pulled both straps tight, then slung the rifle over his shoulder. "The meadow had deer trails. Let's go back and go hunting. And keep that jacket out of sight until we need it. It's a neon sign."

"Just like that? Shouldn't we plan it out or something?"

"It's planned. Shoot. Prop. Drape. Hide."

"We don't want to rush into this." Jared's stomach was twisting like a pail full of worms, writhing in a way that had nothing to do with hunger. "I mean—"

"Your idea, *Moniyaw.* No backing out. Let's go."

"You keep calling me that. What does it mean?"

"What do you *think* it means?" A sneer accompanied the reply.

"I think all sorts of things. It starts at *jerk,* and gets worse from there."

Irritation squinted Kyle's eyes, then eased. "You keep thinking."

"Seriously? You aren't going to tell me?"

With a shrug, Kyle strode back into the forest, forcing

Jared to follow. As he walked, he took off his jacket, stuffed it under his gray T-shirt, and stepped around some stinging nettle. They walked for what seemed like an hour. Kyle moved more cautiously as they continued. Finally he held up his hand, pointed to some underbrush and rolled out his steps, heel to toe, to reach their cover. Jared copied him and squatted under some low-hanging spruce branches an arm's length from Kyle.

The clearing was empty except for the ghostly campfire on the far side. Kyle's kokum wasn't there, just the flames that danced but gave off no light. The sky looked like someone had tried and failed to erase it. A faint haze lightened the blue. Jared's eyes ached. The haze, he realized, was smoke. That forest fire Kyle had pointed out.

Kyle fished two bullets from the pack and tucked one into his breast pocket. He cocked the rifle bolt up, slid it back, loaded one bullet, pushed the bolt forward and down. He settled with one knee up, one in the mossy ground. The rifle rested across his knee, the barrel pointed toward the meadow.

Eyes forward, he whispered, "Watch. Don't move."

Immediately, an itch started behind Jared's ear. The more he tried to ignore it, the worse it itched. Finally, he tilted his head sideways in slow motion, then rubbed his ear, equally slowly, against his shoulder. Straightened.

As time wore on, weariness rose up like the fog had the night before. Higher, higher, until Jared was struggling to keep his eyes open. The fog blurred his vision. His thoughts.

- ———— -

When he woke, the first thing he noticed was that the shadows had moved. A lot. With his phone turned off he didn't know what time it was, but he guessed mid-afternoon. His stomach grumbled and Kyle, who looked sleepy, too, handed him half a piece of bannock. Jared nibbled it, trying to trick his stomach into thinking it was massive.

Bannock eaten, they resettled into stillness. After forever, or maybe forty minutes, movement on the far side of the meadow made Jared stiffen. His first thought was *Wîhtiko,* and his heart thudded as he wondered what the creature looked like. The tension eased slightly when two deer entered the clearing. They approached, pausing every few steps to graze the wild grasses. This place, Jared thought, was a deer's fast food restaurant. Their ears constantly twitched toward sounds. All Jared could hear was buzzing insects.

From the corner of his eye, he noticed Kyle raising the rifle off his knee and toward his shoulder in slow motion, the way a competition diver on the tower raises his arms to pause at right angles to his body before he raises them above his head. The glacial movements were part of the diver's mental preparation, part of gathering his focus so nothing existed except him, the tower, and the coming dive.

Jared pulled out his phone with the same studied movements. He opened the camera function. Muted the phone. Zoomed in, took a picture. There were two deer in the photo. No mysteriously empty meadow.

The deer were halfway across the meadow, tails and ears

flicking. Their tawny coats gleamed under the sun's attention. Birds twittered, a soundtrack to the surreal feeling growing in Jared. Everything was about to change. For better or worse. He wanted to jump up, to yell at the deer to escape.

But if he scared off the deer, their only option would be running. On and on, until they collapsed. Maybe this was some kind of Cree purgatory and he'd landed in it because he'd died on Cree land, and *Wîhtiko* was their torturer, assigned to chase but never catch them. And maybe the jet had killed Kyle when it had crashed—talk about wrong place, wrong time—so that's why they were in this mess together.

Jared had obviously zoned out, because now the rifle sat snug against Kyle's shoulder. He was the diver on the tower, his whole being focused on this one moment. This single twitch of the trigger finger. Jared watched Kyle instead of the deer. The deliberate positioning of his hands, one on the stock behind the trigger, one on the rounded end of the wood where it curved up to meet the barrel. His head beside the rifle butt, his near eye in line with the barrel. His finger on the trigger guard. His shoulders rose, fell, rose, fell. Stopped.

The finger shifted to the trigger. But instead of twitching, the finger slowly, so slowly, squeezed.

Crack!

7

Dinner

Jared's body jerked. The rifle shot echoed around the meadow, into the sky, and away. Kyle ejected the spent cartridge, loaded the second bullet. Rose. He tapped Jared's thigh with his toe. "We've got to move fast."

Jared scanned the meadow, saw one peanut-colored mound. He scrambled to his feet and hurried after Kyle. He hung back, reluctant to see death, then slid his foot forward and leaned toward the deer on the ground. Except for the bloody hole behind its front leg, it looked alive, open eyes black and glistening.

Reason #6 for not being friends: he can kill things.

Kyle crouched and laid his hand on its head. Whispered something. He looked up. "Help me. Quick." He lifted the deer's front quarters. "*Wîhtiko* will probably come from the hill, so the deer's back should face that way."

The why of what they were doing came crashing back. Jared's neck hairs prickled. He stumbled onto one knee, helping Kyle maneuver the deer into an awkward sitting position— front legs propping its torso upright, head sagging onto its chest. It started to fall over and Jared lunged to stop it. A clock was ticking down inside his head. His hands shook as he arranged the head so it didn't move. *Tick, tick, tick.* The velvet soft ear, still warm, contrasted with the smells of blood and deer musk. Jared gagged as he pulled the blue coat from under his T-shirt. He dropped it, scooped it up. *Ticktickticktick.*

Momentary understanding flashed through Jared's mind, a memory from elementary school, maybe, of how the native tribes of long ago had lived as part of an unending circle. How they had used what nature gave them. Like they were doing with this deer, trading its death for their life. If it worked.

Kyle held out his hand. Jared tossed him the jacket. They draped it over the deer's back and tucked the sleeves around its legs to hold the jacket in place. The deer was still warm and Jared half expected it to leap up and bound away. *It was alive. I took its picture. We killed it.*

"This is crazy." Jared spoke quietly, more to himself. Or the deer.

"It is, but at least we're making a move, using a pawn to lure the king from his lair."

Chess. Jared's father had taught him to play, and the king wasn't the most powerful player. He moaned. "Don't tell me *Wîhtiko* has a queen."

"Not that I know of." Kyle picked up his rifle and motioned.

They retreated into the forest as far as they could possibly go and still see the deer, and knelt on a plush carpet of needles under a fan of spruce boughs. The evergreen scent was so strong it almost masked their sweat.

Minutes ticked by. Jared pulled out his phone and switched on the camera again. The needles' squared edges became uncomfortable. Quietly, slowly, Kyle pointed in the direction of the hill. An instant later, Jared heard the cracking and breaking of limbs, someone charging through the forest. Birds stopped singing. Jared remembered how Kyle had relaxed by the creek when he'd heard birds. And how absolute silence had made him hyper alert, like a silent siren warning of danger. Mouth dry, Jared tried to swallow. His ears were seashore caves and the tide of his pulse rushed in, thundering and booming with an underlying hiss that built with each breath. Above them, a squirrel scampered deeper into the forest. He wanted to follow it.

A creature appeared a dozen steps from the deer. Jared's eyes bulged. Even at a distance, the tattered clothing of this vaguely human, skeletal creature didn't hide the roped muscles that twisted and flexed up its limbs. One wide hand extended toward the blue-clad decoy, exposing finger stubs, raw and red-tipped. As if the ends had been chewed off in a fit of hunger. Jared swallowed bile and squinted at its face.

The mouth was a gaping hole. Pieces of lip flapped against a bony chin. Sunken eyes peered from bony caves. Nostrils flared wide. The dangling strips of lip waved as its mouth yawned open. Jared couldn't look away, fascinated by the red-stained teeth and blackened tongue. *This is* Wîhtiko?

He remembered his phone and took a picture. It showed the creature and the dead deer. He inhaled the stink of his rising fear. That thing was as real as the meadow, as the deer. As real as them. *We are so screwed.*

Jared wrenched his gaze to Kyle, who was slack-jawed. Fear pelted down like sleet, skated over skin with sharp blades slicing into ragged composure. Kyle shook his head vigorously, as if he could see Jared was about to give voice to fear.

Jared folded over and touched his forehead to the spruce needles. Worked to slow his breathing. Kyle clamped onto the back of Jared's neck. He jerked up like a marionette. Eyes wide, he expected to see the monster charging at them. But it was focused on that electric blue coat. Freaking neon sign, just like Kyle had said. When it moved, it covered the dozen steps to the deer so fast that Jared almost fell backwards in surprise. Would have if not for Kyle's grip.

It lunged.

With the ferocity of a hungry lion, the creature ripped through the coat, through the hide, into flesh. Blood and muscle and bits of neon blue spattered in all directions. Except for the choking smell of blood, Jared almost felt as though he was watching a Tarantino movie or bad horror flick. The gore held him spellbound.

The creature straightened, howled out something that almost sounded like, "Whiskey Jack!" Then it re-attacked the mangled remains and continued to gorge itself.

"This is bad," Kyle whispered.

"What?" Jared's whisper was barely louder than his breath.

"Don't you see what's happening?"

Jared squinted at the creature, *Wîhtiko*, stuffed with deer meat, blood running down its chin onto its chest. It still looked impossibly gaunt. Exposed ribs, cave-in stomach. It devoured the deer corpse with amazing speed. Nothing remained of Jared's coat except bloodied ribbons strewn around the deer's remains.

Then Jared saw it too: though still cadaverous, the monster was noticeably taller and wider.

Wîhtiko was growing.

8

Firelight

Kyle tapped Jared's shoulder and they retreated silently, though Jared was sure *Wihtiko* could hear the terror crashing through his veins.

Dream or not. Real or not. *Wihtiko* was growing. And that couldn't possibly be good. Their plan had worked, but not in the way they'd expected. A single word drummed through Jared's skull: *crap, crap, crap.* They both burst into a gallop, then a mad dash. Branches slapped. Tangled weeds grabbed. Everything blurred into smears of green and brown with splotches of blue above.

Jared's legs burned. Air whistled into starving lungs. In his mind a monster the size of a spruce tree pursued him, made him keep running. He was slowing, but so was Kyle. Between one step and the next, his energy disappeared. His toe caught on a root; he fell and rolled to a stop.

Spread-eagled, wheezing, he stared up at the blue sky. A face appeared above him and he startled. Kyle. Jared's eyes slammed shut and he rubbed his aching chest.

"Gotta keep moving." Kyle sounded winded too.

Jared squinted upward and grabbed the offered hand. They didn't stop until darkness fell.

Jared kept lifting his head to squint at the shrouded forest. He felt...something. A presence, maybe, but not a person. The awareness stood his arm hairs at attention.

"You feel it, too, don't you?" Kyle asked.

Jared started. "Feel what?" He swallowed, mouth dry.

"That hill. It's like a shadow inside me. Or a magnet. And you keep looking in its direction."

The hill—that was what he'd been sensing. Now he could see its shape in his mind, and the pull was sharper. The hill haunted their horizon, a magnetic north of sorts. All day Jared had felt its pull, had known where it was by the tug of his interior compass needle, just like Kyle had said. Was it trying to trap them somehow so *Wîhtiko* could catch them? He couldn't bring himself to ask the question.

"I freaking hate this place." Jared poked at their small fire with a stick. Sparks swirled and floated on the updraft, winked out before they reached the ceiling of jittering leaves.

He brushed at the layer of grime on his sneakers, used his thumb to polish the gold stripes so they reflected firelight. The smear of dried mud on his stinging nettle rash itched, but he resisted scratching. Its irritation paled next to his aching muscles.

"The bush, it isn't so bad." Kyle's quiet voice was tight.

"Compared to what? The Antarctic in winter?"

"Or the Sahara in summer. Or the Atlantic during a hurricane. Or Los Angeles during rush hour."

"You've been to L.A.?"

"Nah, but we've got TV. We don't live in Moose Camp year round."

"Where do you live?"

"Little place called Wabasca."

"Never heard of it."

Firelight shadowed a scornful expression. "No surprise."

"Will you stay there when you finish school?" Jared feigned interest to keep from thinking about the wildness surrounding them. A place with no walls, no way to keep monsters away. Jared hunched closer to the fire.

Propped up on one elbow, Kyle reclined on his side. His eyes seemed to absorb light. Jared blinked and flames again reflected in the other teen's eyes. He released a breath he didn't realize he'd been holding.

"Do you care?" Kyle asked.

"About what?"

A snort. "No, I won't stay in Wabasca when I graduate. Kokum, she's set on me going to university."

"University? You?"

"What does *that* mean?" Kyle still reclined, but his body stiffened. "Being First Nations doesn't mean I'm stupid. Stupid comes in all colors." His glare was pointed.

Jared resumed poking the fire. "I didn't mean it that way. I just thought, I don't know, that you peop—that First Nations didn't do the university thing."

"Yeah. You thought we all sat on our reserves and collected welfare."

"No. I didn't think of you at all." Jared gave a half apologetic shrug.

Kyle rose into a cross-legged position and rested his elbows on his knees. "Again, not surprised. The rich white boy never thinks of us, unless he goes downtown and sees a homeless First Nations guy, maybe begging, maybe drunk, maybe passed out. And the white boy thinks, 'Why doesn't he go back to wherever he came from?' Or maybe he thinks the homeless guy is garbage. Not a real person."

"Take a pill, dude."

"Why? I'm part of a dream, right? So click your heels three times and make me disappear. Or imagine my skin growing over my mouth, sealing it off, and maybe it will happen."

"You've got a chip the size of Edmonton on that shoulder."

"And you have a deep, deep well of stupid. Every time you open your mouth it flows out like a spring of stinking water."

Jared glared at him, imagined smooth skin where Kyle's mouth was. No mouth, just dark eyes, straight nose, and square chin. Nothing happened. He touched his own lips but didn't answer. The fire snapped, releasing a puff of spruce scent made more pungent by the heat.

"Ever hear of Chief Dan George?" Kyle's question was flat, a peace offering maybe.

"No. Is that your grandfather?"

"No. He's why Kokum wants me to go to university. He was a Salish band chief, did some acting, too, back in the sixties and seventies when Kokum was young. She loved him, said he was a great teacher. Even met him once. A signed picture of him hangs above the TV."

Kyle watched the fire and Jared watched Kyle. That far-away look entered his eyes, the same one he'd had when he'd started into storytelling mode at the jet and on the hilltop. Now he turned his face toward the hill, his eyes seeming to see it, though trees and darkness blocked the view.

Kyle's voice was low and sing-song. "O Great Spirit, whose voice I hear in the winds, I come to you as one of your many children. I need your strength and your wisdom. Make me strong not to be superior to my brother but to be able to fight my greatest enemy: myself."

A prayer. Jared had never thought of spirits, or any kind of god or gods, but in this place—this crazy dream or spirit world—maybe prayers were what they needed. He remembered *Wîhtiko* ripping into that carcass, shivered, and held his hands toward the fire. The heat licked his palms, tickled his fingertips.

Kyle said, "That prayer, it was Chief Dan George's. Kokum makes everyone in the family memorize it. She lives by his words. He gave a speech, back when Canada turned one hundred. Doubt the white men who invited him liked what he said. Maybe some First Nations didn't, either."

The fire crackled. To the west, an owl hunted. Its shrill *"Rheee!"* skimmed the treetops and swooped into their clearing. Jared cleared his throat. "So? What did he say?"

"That First Nations have to embrace the culture we live in. We need to enter politics, law, education, and medicine." Kyle held Jared's gaze. "We have to beat you at your own game."

"He said that?"

"Close enough. The speech says we have to use the white man's tools of success—education and stuff—and build our people up with them."

"So that means you have to go to university."

Kyle stretched out on his back, hands clasped behind his head, and stared at the sky. "Yeah." He closed his eyes, ending the conversation. A few minutes later he rolled away, back to the flames.

Jared continued to poke at the fire. He added more twigs, wanting it to last longer, though Kyle had said they needed to let it die. He felt safer with the fire, even if Kyle thought they were far enough away from *Wîhtiko*.

Glad of the warm night, Jared curled into a half fetal position facing the fire, one arm crooked under his head as a pillow. Kyle's breathing gained volume and shifted gears. Asleep already.

Reason #7: he falls asleep too freaking fast.

Jared couldn't stop his brain from doing the gerbil run, round and round, never finding answers. Tiny flames danced along the fresh twigs in a hypnotic weaving, twirling ripple. They seemed to pause atop the wood, frozen as if caught in ice. At the same instant Jared heard his name whisper through the trees, delivered by a gust of wind that ruffled his hair and stirred the flames back into motion. Jared stared, afraid to move. Over the gushing current of his pulse he heard his name again and lifted his head.

The breeze pushed smoke into his face. He squeezed his stinging eyes closed, nostrils flaring as the smoky smell mixed with the stink of wet dogs.

Something was there. Watching. His stomach turned to stone, threatened to eject the jerky-like stuff called pemmican that had barely touched his growling hunger. He forced his eyes open to slits. A man stood just beyond the firelight, a gray silhouette in the shadows.

Jared started to sit up. The man strode into the darkness. Jared clamped onto Kyle's ankle and shook it. Kyle was sitting, knife in hand, before Jared could pull his hand away.

"It's just me," he whispered, then pointed. "A guy was there, watching us. He walked away before I could say anything."

"What kind of guy?" Kyle sheathed his knife.

"I couldn't tell. He was in shadow." Skepticism carved into Kyle's brow as Jared stood, brushed dust and bits of grass off his jeans. "I'm not imagining it. We have to find him." He stepped around the low fire and studied the darkness. It was a blackout curtain, revealing nothing.

Kyle joined him, small unlit flashlight in hand. "Which way did he go?" Kyle struck out in the direction Jared pointed. He could see outlines once they left the fire behind. He stumbled along, wanting to be back in the city where darkness was only a memory.

He ran into Kyle's unmoving back. The smell of wet dog returned and Jared peered around the bigger teen's torso. Kyle flicked on the light.

"I saw a man," Jared whispered. "I swear."

The creature caught in the beam of light was barely thigh high. Its small head was bear-like. Claws shone yellow-white against the ground, like the animal's bared teeth.

"What is it? A badger?" Jared nudged Kyle and slipped to his side. "Your spirit guide or something. Right? If we're in some spirit world wouldn't your guide show up?" Or in a dream, he added silently.

"That's no badger." Kyle's voice vibrated, a bass thrum of unease. He slid one foot back. His free hand pressed against Jared's midsection, forcing him back, too. Kyle whispered, "It's a wolverine."

"Like the X-Men. Cool."

Small black eyes focused on Jared. The wolverine's snout wrinkled more, better exposing fangs. A low growl rumbled from its throat.

"Not cool," Kyle replied and retreated another step, taking Jared with him. "Deadly. Rip out your throat deadly."

As if Kyle's words were an invitation, the wolverine sprang.

A solid mass of muscle slammed into their shoulders, knocking them both off their feet. Kyle's flashlight winked out.

Jared rolled to his hands and knees. He had seen a man. That man had led them to this creature. It didn't make sense. Where was the man?

Hands grabbed him, hauled him up. He struggled, tried to free himself. Kyle's whisper stopped him. "Calm down. You okay?"

"My throat is unripped, if that's what you're asking."

"It headed toward our camp. Let's follow."

"But you said it's deadly."

"Yeah. So why didn't it attack? Something's going on I don't understand."

"That's my life since I met you."

They crept forward, as silent as possible. When Jared asked for light, Kyle refused. He stopped Jared with a hand against his chest. They both sank into a crouch. Through the trees they could see the fire, dying but still throwing enough light to show the wolverine stalking around it, teeth like white needles in the glimmer. It halted with its hindquarters toward them. The fire cast a halo around the brown-black figure. The hair along its spine bristled.

Beyond the fire, someone stepped from the forest. As he advanced, Jared's stomach hardened so tightly that he gasped. Kyle's hand shot out and covered his mouth. This close, *Wihtiko's* grayish skin made Jared think of Gollum from *The Lord of the Rings*. Its torso hung with tattered and stained clothes that might have once been traditional First Nations leggings and shirt.

The face filled Jared with dread. Sunken eyes, flaring nostrils and torn lips framing that horrible gaping mouth that seemed to be slavering. *Wihtiko* radiated hunger, even after gorging on that deer. Its exposed ribs were gaunt. Its skeletal arms reached as if to embrace the wolverine, but it stayed back.

The wolverine dug furiously. Dirt sprayed out behind him onto the fire. It guttered out. The sudden darkness, with nothing more than a sliver of moonlight, left only the gray figure of the ragged monster visible. Jared's pulse slammed in his own ears. He wondered if it could hear them, smell them.

Moisture fled his mouth as it stepped toward the dead fire and Jared realized the wolverine was gone. Rustling branches beside their camp drew the monster's attention. A voice shattered the silence, yelled something in a language Jared didn't know. Then footsteps retreated through the forest. Branches snapped, like someone—or something—was breaking things on purpose.

Wîhtiko lunged into the forest to chase the runner. Away from the camp. Crashing and moaning and thumping after... after whom? The man Jared had seen? The one who had led them to the wolverine?

"They're gone." Jared's breathing eased.

Kyle hauled him up. "We can't stay here," he whispered.

Jared knocked the large hand off his sleeve. "I know."

9

Fight

Running, running. Never stopping. Leaves slap his face. Branches catch at his jacket, grab him. Roots trip him. He scrambles up. Runs.

Behind him, a loping, grunting creature gets closer. Breath heaves. Branches snap. Closer.

Roaring engulfs him. Spins him around. A shadowy creature leaps out of a black night. Strikes his chest. Pins him with a painful jarring. White fangs drip saliva onto his face. Ebony eyes flare with hunger. The jaw yawns open. Teeth sink into his forehead and chin.

- ——— -

Jared woke with a gasp. Flung himself away from the nightmare. His hand splashed into water, and the chill finished waking him. On his elbows, he leaned over a pool, barely noticing the ripples of wavering reflection, green and blue.

He splashed some water on his face, cupped some and drank. Started to cough. The water tasted stony, like he imagined concrete might taste. He looked around.

The tiny pool was created by the backwash of a stream's currents. Forest leaned close over both sides of the water, barely letting sunlight reach the ground. Jared rolled onto his back and stared at tantalizing bits of blue.

Slowly the night's memories returned. They had fled for a large part of it; adrenaline had pushed them farther than Jared had imagined he could go. When they stopped, Jared's exhaustion had plunged him into a bottomless, near-comatose sleep.

Jared rolled back to splash more water on his face, drank despite the flinty taste. His stomach growled, unsatisfied with water. The morning chill stippled his arms.

Behind him, a throat cleared. He jerked around. Kyle crouched by a fire, his eyes crinkled with silent laughter. "Jumpy this morning."

"Almost as jumpy as you were last night."

Kyle focused on tending the flames. "You were squirming lots before you woke."

"We ran most of the night, then I kept running in my dreams."

"Me, too. No dreamcatchers out here."

Jared shrugged his incomprehension.

"You gotta know what dreamcatchers are. They're everywhere." Kyle squinted at him in apparent disbelief. "They're round, look kind of like spider webs with feathers hanging down. They catch bad dreams and only let good ones through."

"So they're a...decoration?"

"Maybe to you." Kyle huffed quietly and dropped his gaze.

Jared inched closer to see what Kyle was cooking. The smell of fish turned his stomach.

He inhaled deeply, let the gross scent fill his nostrils. His dream slithered back into his mind. The wolverine had drooled into his face, but there hadn't been any smell. The slithering turned to a tightness that wrung his thoughts as understanding slowly crept in. Last night he'd stood two yards away from the animal and had gagged on its dog-skunk stench. He scowled at the fish fillets skewered on a stick that Kyle rotated over the low fire, scowled more when the smell made his stomach tighten and rumble simultaneously. A riptide tore him away from the safety he'd clung to—the hope, the wish that this was all a dream. But...the *smell*.

Horror clutched at Jared's throat, his stomach, his limbs. He leapt up and back. Sprayed gravel onto the fire.

"Whoa!" Kyle's arm shot out. His hand shielded the fish. "This is our breakfast."

Jared couldn't stop shaking his head. "No. I shouldn't be able to smell it." He backed away some more.

"Of course you can smell it. That's what happens when you cook stuff." Kyle scanned the trees. "So long as nothing else smells it. It's cooked. Let's eat it quick."

"You don't understand." Jared pointed with a shaking finger. "I can *smell* it." He spun, dropped to his knees by the pool. Bent over, clutching his stomach. "I shouldn't. Be able. To s-smell." Panic hitched his breathing. *It can't be real. It can't.*

A hand clamped onto his shoulder. Jared tried to jerk away but Kyle held him down.

"I think I'm going crazy." Jared breathed through his mouth, unable to get enough oxygen. He sucked in as deeply as he could. "Can't. Breathe." His fingers tingled painfully. Spots danced on the edges of his vision. He gasped repeatedly. Fish out of water. Fish. He could smell the fish. Gasped more urgently.

Kyle shook him. "You're hyperventilating or something. Kokum, help me. Paper bag. No bag." Kyle stripped off his jacket and draped it over Jared's head. "Breathe. Count to five, and breathe slowly."

From the dark interior of the jacket all Jared heard was that deep voice. "Breathe slowly." The words stretched out, slower and slower. Jared found himself matching his inhalation and exhalation to the words. "B-rea-thhhe s-looow-leeee."

The panic receded. Jared plucked at the hand holding the jacket over him. "Need fresh air."

Kyle pulled the jacket away and Jared gulped the cool morning air. Kyle watched him for a moment, then retreated and uprooted the stick with its fish fillets that he'd jabbed into the ground. He kicked dirt and rocks over the fire and returned to sit by Jared, who stared at the fish. It smelled a bit charred.

His breathing started to speed up again and he pulled his

T-shirt over his head. This time he noticed the odor of stale sweat. They'd been out here two nights. His own stink was possibly worse than fish. He lifted his head.

Kyle broke the stick in half and handed one skewered fillet to Jared. "Want to tell me what that was about?"

"No."

Kyle exhaled loudly. "Look, *Moniyaw,* you need to understand. I don't usually talk to your type. I'm trying..."

He picked off a piece of fish and ate it. Some sort of struggle rippled across his features—anger, or maybe frustration, ebbing and flowing like an ocean tide. He broke off a piece of stick and tossed it away, then continued, "I'm trying because Kokum would expect me to help. But you... you're everything I don't like about whites."

Jared turned his stick over and over. "So you hate me because I'm rich? Because I live in a nice place and have nice things?"

"You're too puny to hate." Kyle squinted into the distance for a moment. "There's this old country song that says something about rich kids who think they're better because they're better off. That's you. You think because you were born in the city, and born rich, it makes you better than me."

"I. Don't—" Jared snapped his mouth shut, rubbed at the stripe on his runner as a scowl crawled across his forehead.

"Better eat your fish, *Moniyaw.*"

"Don't like fish."

"It might be the only thing we eat all day. If you don't want it, I'll eat it."

Jared eyed the outstretched hand but didn't relinquish his fish.

"Is that why the smell freaked you out? Because you don't like to eat it?" Kyle popped a big chunk of the fillet into his mouth and chewed.

Jared licked his lips and nibbled a tiny morsel. It was blissfully tasteless, but hard to swallow. He shook his head.

"Tell me. I gotta know if I can trust you to not freak out again."

"I don't know if you can." Jared squeezed his eyes shut. "You'll laugh, but I realized that I can smell things. I woke up from a nightmare with that wolverine drooling into my face. I couldn't smell it. But I could smell it last night in the forest. And I could smell this stupid fish." He searched Kyle's puzzled features. "Can you smell things when you dream?"

A shrug. "Never thought about it."

Jared ran his finger over the ridges of fish flesh. It felt so real. *Smelled* so real. Maybe comas had deeper dreams, ones that included smells. *Please let that be real.* But the wish crumbled under the growing certainty in his gut. "If I can smell things then this"—he waved with his free hand—"this might be real. That thing we saw yesterday might be real." He remembered the picture he'd taken of it and a tremor ran down his arms.

"Start thinking it's not real and you'll be filling its belly."

Jared ate a larger piece of fish, glad it was bland. He squinted at the stream and the forest beyond. "If you die in a dream, do you die in real life?"

Fish eaten, Kyle stabbed his stick into the damp earth

and stared unblinking at Jared for a long moment. Then he shook his head, emptied the canteen over the fire, refilled it, and hooked it to his backpack. He sniffed the air. "We should be on the move, *Moniyaw*."

Jared stood. "I'm really tired of you calling me puny, stupid, Moonie-whatever. If you won't tell me what it means, stop calling me it."

"*Moniyaw* isn't an insult. It just means white man."

"And if I called you 'brown man,' you'd flatten me." Jared threw up his hands in mock surrender. "Whatever. Call me anything you want."

The trees crowded the edge of the stream and they set out single-file. A few times Jared's foot slipped on rocks and he barely avoided stepping in the water. With Kyle leading the way and not looking back, as usual, Jared took out his iPhone and powered it up with no success.

He returned the cell to his pocket. "That man last night yelled something. Did you understand him?"

"He spoke Cree. I think he said, 'Hello my brother. How are you?'"

"He called Wîh—that monster his brother? It has a brother?"

"Don't think so. Saying 'my brother' is common between Cree, when we're speaking Cree."

"If following him led us to the wolverine, does that means the wolverine is his pet?"

"Not even a Cree warrior could have a wolverine as a pet. It's almost a miracle to see one, never mind to be that close and not be attacked." Kyle rounded a corner and called a halt. He studied the area, behind and front. "Something's out there."

Jared felt like a discarded poolside towel. Going berserk had left him exhausted, wrung out. The knowledge that this place was real sped up his heartbeat and breathing. His hard-won calm frayed at the possibility of being followed. "How can you tell?"

Kyle shrugged. "I saw a shadow moving under the trees when we took the corner."

"Not—?"

"I don't think so."

To keep panic from rising again, Jared latched onto his hatred of this place. Freaking trees hiding freaking animals, every turn hiding something that wanted to trip you, sting you, attack you. "Why would something follow us?"

"Maybe we smell like dinner." Kyle grinned.

"Not funny. How can you even think about joking right now?"

Kyle shrugged.

"We have to figure this out, not joke. What'll get us back home?"

"Don't know. Kokum said run. Maybe we have to get away from the thing we woke."

"What is this? Harry Potter? Avoiding the-one-who-shall-not-be-named? Should we call your monster Voldemort as a codename?"

"It might be a Cree legend, but you woke it up. I think that makes it *your* monster."

"Screw that. You said it was your fault."

"For not stopping you from climbing the hill." Kyle poked Jared's chest. "But all of this is your fault, *Moniyaw.*"

The thick disdain made the word pure insult this time. Jared's vision blurred. He shoved the taller teen, barely backing him a step. "Just because you could pulverize me doesn't mean I have to live with your poking. You're always poking. Just leave me the hell alone."

Kyle shifted his backpack and sneered. "Leave you alone? Gladly. You, you're a whiny, panicky little asshole who'll get us both killed. Always tiptoeing like that stripe on those fancy leather shoes is real gold. Always checking your phone to see if it's working even though we're in a world without cell towers. You trust it more than me."

Jared's limbs vibrated. His fists clenched. "Why *should* I trust you? Do you even know where you're leading us?"

"Away from danger. I'm following water, hoping to find help. Out here, drinking water is life. If someone's around, they'll be near water."

"That guy last night wasn't near water. You know piss all."

"And what does the runt who wasn't even in Boy Scouts know about living in the bush? Boot up that phone. Maybe you can download an app for wilderness survival."

"Leave me to it. If you can bring yourself to risk upsetting your precious granny."

"At least I can tell Kokum I tried to save your hide." He leaned close and whispered, "*Ekosi, Wîhtiko*-snack." Kyle shifted his backpack and rifle to the other shoulder and strode away. He disappeared around a crook in the stream.

Jared gaped. Disbelief eroded his anger. He pivoted slowly, scanned the treetops, the stream. Quiet enveloped him, broken only by the water's gurgle.

He stumbled to a fallen tree that lay parallel to the stream and plopped onto the higher end. It gave a little under his weight and he cringed, but exhaustion pounded him and he hardly cared if it collapsed in a rotten pile. He shifted and swiped at one side of his butt, glad he couldn't see what his jeans looked like from behind.

As he sat—feeling numb, hands braced on the cool bark, gaze on the gold stripe of one sneaker—birdsong started in the trees above him. *Chicka-dee-dee-dee. Chicka-dee. Chicka-dee-dee-dee.*

His thoughts shriveled from the realization that he was completely alone.

Down the log, a flash of gray and brown made him tense. His shoulders relaxed when he saw a tiny bird with a feathery brown cap. Its black beak and eyes were hidden by black bands that reminded Jared of the kind worn by cartoon burglars. The bird pecked at the log for a few moments then disappeared into the trees in another flurry, its hunger apparently satisfied.

Wîhtiko-snack.

At least the bird could fly. How could he escape a monster when he didn't even know where he was? Jared searched the sky. The trees leaned over him.

He powered up his cellphone and frowned at the picture he'd taken of the monster. It was real. It was real and out there and Kyle had left him to be its snack. He moved toward the stream. No signal. Of course there was no signal. He opened the map icon anyway. When he typed his address into the route search bar it asked if he wanted to use his current location as a starting point. He agreed. The little arrow circled and circled. The app informed him it couldn't connect to a network.

Fury exploded again. Jared hurled the phone onto the stones, stomped on it and swore. Kept swearing, louder and louder. Hammered the phone with his heel, an exclamation point after each word. He hurled the largest fragment into the forest.

Jared dropped to his knees and fell silent. Air stuttered in and out. His throat ached. He leaned toward the stream and scooped handfuls of water to his mouth. Most of it ran between his fingers and up his arm. He bent over, slurped in the cold liquid, then splashed his face and sat back on his heels.

The bits of plastic and glass mocked him. A deep well of stupid. Not only had he trashed his phone, he had screamed his location to everything in hearing distance.

He still didn't move. "Pointless," he whispered. "Dying *beyond nowhere,* in some other dimension. No one will ever know what happened."

In their world, headlines would read, "Diamond Millionaire's Son Disappears." They would search—for months, years—but no trace would be found. They'd assume he'd sunk in a bog, or been eaten by an animal. They'd never know they were almost right. Eaten by a legend.

Jared remembered a party back in that other world—one that had been held not too long after a teen across town was killed in a car accident. After a few beers, he and his friends had started discussing the best way to go. They'd almost pissed themselves laughing at the fake obituaries they invented. Shawn's had been the best, something about a zombie hockey player checking him from behind then dragging him to the penalty box to snack on while serving its penalty.

Wihtiko-snack. "I'm not even a full meal, just a snack," Jared muttered. "What an obit that'll make." He scanned up and down the stream, half hoping to see the one person who had tried to help him. "Don't leave, Kyle. I hate being alone."

Stones dug into his shins and ankles. Jared barely felt them as he stared in the direction of the hill and struggled to keep dread away.

A bear ambled out of the forest and stopped mid-stream. *Crap.* It swung its head back and forth, smelling something. Jared smelled only spruce and a hint of smoke. The bear faced him, and he realized the bear was interested in one smell: his.

Jared rose in slow motion. The bear stood on its hind legs, front legs dangling, and stared at him. Its black eyes made him recall the vice-principal's beady glare when he'd caught Jared skipping classes at the mall. A glare that meant trouble.

Sliding his foot back, Jared caught his heel on a rock and flailed his arms to regain his balance. The bear woofed, dropped to all fours with a splash, and advanced toward Jared. A determined gait. Panic pounced on Jared like football players on a fumbled ball.

He wheeled and ran.

10

Curiosity

Jared bolted in the direction Kyle had gone. Behind him, the rhythmic lope of the bear grew louder with every second.

His senses narrowed to two sounds: running and breathing, his and the bear's. Wheezes. Cracking of pebbles. Splashes. Grunts.

He sprinted around a bend and spotted Kyle on a rock, head hanging low. He yelled, "Bear! Run!" Kyle rose, rifle in hand. Jared glanced back—and tripped. He sprawled onto gravel and twigs. Dread flung over him like a net. He curled up, covered his head with his arms, squeezed his eyes shut.

"*Maskwa! Nitotem!*" Kyle's voice rang out as he kept repeating two words: *maskwa* and *nitotem*.

Jared began shaking. Mouth a desert, he wanted to tell Kyle to save himself, but his lips were glued together. Kyle's voice dropped low. The words blended with the tumbling stream, which seemed to laugh at Jared. He forced his eyes open. No bear loomed over him. He zeroed in on Kyle's camouflaged back and wide-legged stance. Both his arms extended toward the sky, and the rifle teetered in his right hand.

Kyle continued to speak in Cree. Jared peered between Kyle's legs and spotted the bear standing upright like when it had first noticed him, front legs hanging slack by its sides. It seemed to be listening to Kyle, head tilted to the side like a person concentrating.

Whatever Kyle said seemed to work. The bear dropped onto all fours and lumbered toward the forest. By the first tree, it paused and looked back at Kyle, who continued to stand with hands aloft, the rifle now rocking. The bear slipped soundlessly into the forest.

Kyle didn't move for a minute. His arms lowered and his whole body sagged to the ground. He splashed water over his head. His shoulders rose and fell, rose and fell until stillness settled over him. He stood and remained unmoving for another minute before he turned.

Acute embarrassment rolled over Jared when he realized he hadn't moved from his fetal position. Kyle rested his rifle on his shoulder, walked over and nudged Jared's knee with the toe of his boot. "Are you completely clueless? Running's the worst thing you could've done."

Jared scrambled away from the contempt and collapsed onto the rock Kyle had occupied when Jared had first raced around the bend.

Reason #8: he isn't freaked out by bears like a normal

person would be.

Kyle followed. Jared forced his cracked lips open. "I can't take this." He hunched over, rubbed his knees with aching hands. He picked at a small rip in his jeans with quivering fingers. "I. Don't. Belong. Here."

"*Moniyaw*, calm down. The bear was young, small. Just curious I think."

"It looked big."

"That's because you, you're small, too."

"You had your rifle. I...Why didn't you shoot it?"

"*Maskwa* is our brother and means many things to the Cree. It's one thing to hunt a bear, but we'd never harm a bear unless we had no choice."

Jared tried to swallow. "But it might come back. Attack us." Kyle's skeptical expression needled him. "Why weren't you scared?"

"Who said I wasn't? But it was just following you, so I stretched tall and explained we're its friends."

"You still *did* something. You didn't run."

"Running doesn't usually help."

Jared kicked a spray of pebbles. "Then why are we running from that monster?" He glared at Kyle.

The other teen shrugged and cast a worried frown toward the hill. "Since our feeding plan didn't work, I didn't know what to do. Kokum said to run."

Jared's hands curled into fists. He flattened them and rubbed his thighs, as if he could massage calm back into his body. "I think I'm going crazy. One second I'm so freaking scared. The next I'm so angry I could hit something."

"Yeah, I heard that anger." Kyle snorted quietly as he sank into a crouch and balanced himself by planting the rifle stock on the ground. "It sounded like you were killing something." A question mark curved his eyebrows.

"My phone. I killed my phone."

A smile crinkled out from Kyle's eyes but didn't touch his mouth. "Because of what I said about downloading an app?"

Jared stopped rubbing his throbbing hands and rested them, palms up, on his knees. Red welts marked both palms. Kyle was talking to him in the quiet voice again, like he had used on the bear to keep it calm. Like he was a kid having a temper tantrum at the edge of a cliff and needed to be coaxed away. He shook his head. "I powered the phone up again. Stupid, right? And when it wouldn't connect to a network, the idea of being a, a snack for...I don't know. I flipped. Then the bear came and I thought I was going to be bear food instead."

"So you ran."

"I'm not like this at home. Here I'm useless."

"You really are."

Jared cringed. "Thanks. That makes me feel much better."

"You want me to lie?"

A frown dropped over Jared's brow. He almost said *yes*, then a thought occurred to him. "I thought you'd left me to die. Why were you so close?"

"Because I only got this far before Kokum slapped me down."

"How? Is she here now?" He scanned the area, looking for a ghostly figure.

"No, but her teaching's inside me. Just like your parents' teachings are inside you."

"What teachings?" How to shop like a pro? Obsess over work? How to ignore your kid and not give him any truly useful advice? Like how to avoid being chased by a bear.

Kyle eyed him for a moment. "I'd say you've learned to think of yourself first. And to believe that a big bank account and fancy things make you special."

Jared snatched up a stone and chucked it at a tree. Missed. He scooped up a second stone and felt a crack that marred one side. Cracked like his family. Dad spent all his time building up his diamond mine and his bank account. Mom spent all hers running her travel agency and holidaying with her new husband. Even his grandparents were across the country. Alone was his default mode. No wonder he hated it. But he also hated Kyle judging him.

"You don't know anything. I was on my way to spend a month with my dad. He loves my visits. Loves spending time with me and teaching me about his business." His parents could never tell when he was lying, but Kyle looked skeptical.

"I didn't say anything about where you were going. Let's walk." Kyle retrieved his backpack and slung it over his shoulder as he studied the area. His lips pressed together. As he turned away, a shadow swooped across his features.

Still fingering the stone, Jared followed Kyle as he started downstream, glad that there had been no talk of leaving him behind. Kyle could call him anything he wanted so long as they stuck together. Although, *whiny, panicky little asshole* was harsh. Little, fine; panicky, maybe; but the rest? Jared dropped the stone and marched behind the broad back.

Jared kicked a rock that skittered into the stream. His feet were sore, especially the back of his right heel. He scowled at his sneakers' leather toes, now mapped with fine scratches. Their flat soles weren't made for this.

Kyle held up his hand to call a stop at another curve in the waterway. He did his usual scan of the area, followed by his usual silence. He remained facing the way they'd come, frown firmly in place. Jared only saw the stream cutting through a forest. Blue sky. A photographer might think it was a nice picture, but he didn't see anything interesting.

Kyle faced the cursed hill. "We ran north last night, I think. The creek's been taking us back west-northwest. We'll come to the Peace if we follow it far enough."

"The Peace?"

"River. Don't you know Alberta geography?"

"But if we're in a spirit world, does it have the same geography?"

Kyle studied the water, worry flitting across his face. Jared suspected he had scored a point but it didn't give him any satisfaction. His nerves jittered as he fingered the compass in his pocket.

The wind rattled the treetops. Jared smelled spruce and smoke and his own sweat. A rancid mixture.

To the east, where the stream became indistinct and the trees merged into a wall of dark green, a distant puff of black rose into the sky. "What's that?" Jared shielded his eyes from the sun. "A smoke signal or something?"

Kyle remained silent as the blackness dispersed but didn't disappear. Some of it floated toward them. In a few minutes, Jared could tell it was birds, not smoke. Black birds. As they flew overhead, the urgent swish of their wings seemed to whisper a warning.

"Ravens," Kyle said. Expression solemn, he squinted in the direction they'd come from.

Only half a dozen ravens had flown overhead. "What would such a big group of them be doing in one place?"

"Something dead maybe. They were eating when something scared them away." Kyle got out his canteen and took a drink. He passed it to Jared, who swigged some warm water. Kyle refilled it from the stream. "Normally a raven will retreat, watch the bigger predator eat its fill, then return to finish eating when the carcass is free again."

Jared wiped his suddenly dry mouth. "You don't think that man we saw last night was caught by—And it left him and now it's come back to, to, *finish eating*." His stomach squirmed.

Kyle clipped the canteen back on the backpack. "What I think is, we should keep moving."

Jared's feet ached at the thought. But his gut screamed at him to do what the birds had done: fly.

11

Shelter

With each step, a razor blade of pain slashed Jared's heels, his right worse than his left. He wanted to peel off his shoes and socks and soak in the cool stream. He didn't suggest it.

The tenseness in Kyle's shoulders signaled urgency. And the memory of the ravens lifting into the air like a belch of black smog made it feel as if something equally black and very evil lurked somewhere behind them. Something besides that damn hill. Thinking about *evil* in any way other than a descriptor for a horror movie was unsettling. Now scenes from those corny horror flicks filled him with dread.

He strove to keep his mind blank and keep up with Kyle's pace beside the stream, a knee-high dirt bank beside them. It seemed oddly urban: a wall, a walkway, a road (stream).

Something black flickered in the corner of his eye, a

shadow skimming between the trees off to their left. It disappeared. Jared had been lagging but now sped forward to catch Kyle. When he mentioned the shadow, Kyle said, "Don't panic, *Moniyaw*. It was probably a deer."

"I said black. Even I know deer aren't black."

"In the shadows under the trees anything except a polar bear will look black."

"Even *Wîh*—the monster?"

Kyle scanned the underbrush with worry curving his brow. "I...think it would come straight at us if it was this close. It doesn't mess around. So let's go."

They kept a brutal pace. Pain radiated from Jared's heels, but twice more he spotted movement in the trees, and each time it spurred him forward and temporarily helped him ignore his feet.

"Is it getting darker? Feels like we've been walking for days. Are we going to have to spend the night in the open?" He suppressed a shudder.

"Yeah. We need to find someplace to hole up." Kyle kept walking.

The only part of Jared's body complaining louder than his feet was his stomach. He had been hungry before, the kind of hungry that comes from a hard swim practice, but it was always easily satisfied. Shower, get dressed, get a ride to the nearest fast-food joint, eat. His stomach started grinding painfully.

As he trudged along, he kept looking back, expecting to see the shadow again. A branch slapped him in the face. "Lay off, Kyle. Can't you—"

"Shh. Sorry, okay?" Kyle pointed. The stream melted into a marsh that pushed the trees back and exposed a ceiling of dusky blue sky. The spruce trees bordering the marsh were scraggly and grayish, with taller, darker trees behind them. Barren poles broken off a meter or two above the marsh grasses stuck up here and there in the open expanse. Still water dotted with light green algae was visible in spots.

An elbow rammed Jared's upper arm. "Ouch. What?"

Kyle pointed again. This time, Jared saw regularly spaced mounds to the left hugging a narrow band of dry ground above the marsh. "What are they?" he asked.

"Moss houses. An old kind of woodland Cree lodge." Kyle retreated along the stream and beckoned Jared. He drank long from the canteen, refilled it, drank again and gave it to Jared.

The cool water almost made Jared's stomach rebel. He wanted solid food. But after a few swigs, his stomach settled with a gurgle.

Kyle refilled the canteen again and waded across the knee-deep stream. "Come on."

Jared frowned down at his shoes. Water would ruin the suede, and probably the leather, too. Kyle waited on the other side of the water, looking impatient. Jared took a breath.

He plunged through the water.

- ——— -

Kyle and Jared crouched between two spruce trees and studied the village of seven earthen mounds.

Moss houses, Kyle had called them. They had a teepee shape, but were shorter and broader. Poles stuck out of the roofs in a crisscrossing circle. There were more poles than in any picture of teepees Jared had ever seen. He guessed they formed walls that supported the outer layers of mud and moss—a Cree version of plaster.

Each moss house had a welcome mat of what looked like spruce branches in front of a doorway that was almost rectangular, narrower at the top. But there were no signs that the houses were occupied.

"Where is everyone?" Jared whispered.

"Maybe the villagers know what woke up and they ran." Kyle shifted, using the planted rifle stock to balance himself.

"Should we check it out?"

"Us, we've got nothing to lose, so yeah. It'll be dark soon."

Jared shuddered. "It's shelter. That's good."

"We'll scout it out, then decide."

"You mean, you'll decide."

Kyle expelled a loud breath. After a moment of tense silence he faced Jared. Under lowered brows his eyes were black orbs in shadowed caves. "Why is that so hard for you?"

Jared opened his mouth. Closed it. Shrugged.

"White-boy superiority crap."

The vehemence in Kyle's voice surprised Jared. "I-I don't think that's it. I have friends who aren't white." That earned him a sneer. "I'm...used to getting my own way. That's all. I'm usually in charge."

"How does a runt like you get to be boss with guys our age?" Kyle's eyebrows rose. A sneer entered his voice. "I get it. The fancy clothes. The private jet. You're the richest kid, so everyone sucks up to you."

Jared stood. "This is stupid. Are we checking out the village or not?"

Kyle unfolded himself and stretched. "Yeah. I hit that ball out of the park. So are your friends nice because they like you or because of your deep pockets? Maybe their parents make them suck up to you so they can get in good with your parents."

"Do your friends like you or are they afraid of you? Big freaking goon." Jared's gut was churning.

"I told you I walk away from fights when I can. But if you push too hard, I might make an exception." He leaned in. "Runts like you should learn to not be so mouthy."

"And people like you should learn—"

Kyle snagged Jared's collar and hauled him close. "People. Like. Me? You mean *Indians?*" His expression was fierce.

"N-no," Jared rasped, "I meant—" *Bullies*, he finished silently as Kyle's chokehold tightened.

"Don't talk to me about my people. You have no idea, not one single clue in that insect mind of yours, what it's like to be treated like scum because of your skin color." Kyle's fist had been curling the cloth around Jared's neck tighter and tighter as he spoke.

Heat painted Jared's cheeks. He choked out a faint, "Sorry."

Kyle's hold loosed slightly as he continued to glare with

what felt like lasers of pure hate. Jared's gut recoiled with fear, uncertainty. *I'm not a bad guy. I don't deserve*—A thought sliced through him and he tensed. Eyes wide with realization he whispered, "I *do* know what it's like. It's how you've been treating me since we hiked up that hill."

Kyle blinked. The anger drained from his expression, leaving confusion in its wake. After a moment he dropped his hand, muttered an apology, and stalked toward the moss houses.

Jared rubbed his neck. That comment about his friends liking him for his money had felt like pins jabbed under his fingernails. He had wanted to strike out, but he hadn't expected that harsh reaction to his jab. Jared realized Kyle was right: mostly, he knew nothing about being put down because other people had decided they were better than him. He'd never had anyone refuse him service, or kick him out of a store, or call him down. And he'd never noticed it happening to other people. He'd never paid attention. Never cared.

Kyle stopped to watch some ducks fly overhead. He tracked them with his rifle, then lowered it without shooting. The ducks flew so low over Jared's head that he heard the rapid *whish-whish* of their wings beating the air.

He groaned and his stomach grumbled over the lost roast duck feast. As he picked his way down a beaten path along the edge of the marsh, mosquitoes dive-bombed him. The first ones he'd noticed since they'd entered this other world. He swore when he realized he'd stopped trying to even pretend this was a dream.

He reached Kyle. "Why didn't you shoot one of those ducks? I'm starving."

Kyle shrugged. "Too noisy."

Jared cast an uneasy glance in the direction of the hill, its crest barely visible over the tops of the trees. Yet it still felt like a giant hunkered in his mind. How far did the sound of a rifle shot carry? Jared shivered and turned his attention to the moss houses.

"Think there's food in those huts?"

Kyle passed him the canteen and they both slaked their thirst. Jared poured a bit in his palm and rubbed it over his face, rinsing away some sweat. Kyle shouldered the rifle. "We should check them out. I'll take the ones on the left, you take those." He pointed to the right.

Jared sniffed. More than his sweat, there was a faintly sour smell he couldn't quite place. It wasn't bad enough to be something rotting, but it was still noticeable. Like slimy lettuce in the crisper. Kyle headed toward the first hut on the left so Jared tentatively approached the doorway closest to him. Its trapezoidal opening was covered by a flap made from animal hide.

His voice croaked. "Anyone home?" No answer. He pushed the hide door aside and let the waning light fill the interior. Walls of skinny poles leaned toward the center. A circle of stones marked a cold fire pit in the middle of the circular hut. Spruce boughs to the right, maybe a bed, were bunched into a jumbled pile. A hide was rolled up near the door. Jared picked it up and retreated. Kyle was already entering his second house.

Jared approached the next house more boldly. It was identical inside, minus the rolled-up hide. At the doorway to the third house, he sniffed again. The smell was stronger, muskier. He pushed aside the animal skin curtain and startled when a mouse scuttled past his foot. As the rodent disappeared into the grasses beside the swamp, he wondered what mouse tasted like. "Disgusting," he muttered.

This hut had spruce boughs scattered across the floor. He wedged the rawhide flap between the doorframe and the next pole and stepped inside. The smells of smoke and animal hide choked him as he scanned the interior, then retreated.

He met Kyle but dropped the skin when Kyle tossed something at him, a long-sleeved shirt of deerskin. "Too small for me. Put it on."

Jared pulled the shirt over his head and was instantly warmer. He plucked at the baggy sides and tugged the too-short sleeves. "Better than nothing."

Kyle nodded at the last building. An overpowering stench, worse than wet dog, seemed to radiate from it. Jared covered his mouth to keep from gagging.

"That's rank." Kyle cautiously approached the door flap. He paused on the welcome mat of spruce branches and tilted his head up, then to the side, as if examining something. Jared squinted in the dimming light. The air seemed to waver above the house.

Instead of reaching for the rawhide door, Kyle quietly said, "*Tansi?*"

From inside a voice replied, "*Astam*."

Jared inhaled sharply. Kyle shot him a warning glance and reached out to sweep the door flap aside. Jared lunged and grabbed his arm. "Stop! This is the part of the movie where the idiot walks into the dark basement and gets dismembered."

"What are you talking about?"

"Horror flicks. Dude, you don't want to go in there."

"Get a life, *Moniyaw*."

Kyle wrenched his arm free, bunched the door flap and held it aside. In the moss house, a man sat cross-legged by a low fire, his back stiff, palms resting on his knees. Long hair fell halfway down his chest and he wore traditional clothing. His face was all angles and sharpness, including his assessing gaze.

The man studied Jared, nodded as if he'd seen him before. Worry quivered along Jared's limbs. Where could he have met someone who was so obviously a Cree warrior? Kyle's words popped into his mind. *Not even a Cree warrior could have a wolverine as a pet.* That was it! The stink was wolverine. Maybe Kyle was wrong and this Cree warrior *did* have a pet wolverine. Jared glanced around nervously, expecting to see a black shadow...

Was that what had been following them all day?

Following? Or herding? Would it have attacked them if they'd tried to turn around?

Before Jared could express his misgivings, Kyle entered the moss house, leaving Jared alone in the swelling dark. The evening breeze rattled spruce needles, raked his hair and whispered of his helplessness. Alone in the night.

Possibly with a wolverine watching him this very moment. The breeze wafted around his head again, and seemed to whisper his name.

With a shudder, Jared scooped up the hide he'd dropped and dove through the doorway.

12

Mystery Man

Jared stumbled into the moss house, hide roll clutched to his chest. The Cree warrior eyed him with obvious amusement. The hide wasn't much of a shield but it was all he had.

"Don't worry," Kyle said. "He wouldn't have invited us inside if he'd meant to hurt us."

"He invited us in? Thanks for telling me." Kyle shrugged a single-shouldered apology of sorts. The smell of the smoke did little to mask the stench of the place. Jared asked, "Why pick this hut? Why not one that doesn't stink?"

The warrior listened with a mildly puzzled expression. Jared guessed he couldn't speak English. Kyle didn't respond, either, but studied the warrior intently. The man's buckskin leggings and shirt looked supple, well-worn but not worn out. No embroidery and only short fringes on the leggings.

A breechcloth draped in his lap and moccasin toes poked out from under his legs. A segmented white choker ringed his neck. Jared found it hard to look away from the man's intense gaze. He seemed to miss nothing, not even a nervous licking of lips.

Jared fidgeted by the doorway, his restlessness growing as the silence lengthened. He noticed three piles of spruce boughs with what looked like folded bearskins by each. Was the warrior expecting them? Had he guessed right about the wolverine making sure they ended up here? Unease and the smell churned Jared's stomach, which was roiling from hunger. He slid one foot toward the door flap and fresh air.

"*Pe mitso.*" The warrior opened his palm toward the fire. Though quiet, his voice seemed to fill the space.

Kyle nodded. He lowered his pack and rifle to the floor and crouched, then looked up at Jared. "He invited us to eat."

Jared blinked and for the first time noticed the cooked carcass on a flat rock on the far side of the fire. He dropped to his knees; pain pinched his heels. "What is it? Never mind. I don't care." His mouth watered as Kyle tore a leg off and handed it to him.

He held it under his nose and inhaled deeply. The smell of roast meat momentarily overcame the stench in the hut, and he sank his teeth into the leg. He stared at the carcass as he chewed, thinking maybe it was rabbit, but it could have been skunk or rat for all he cared. The juices dribbled down his chin and neck. He wiped at them with a finger and licked it off.

Kyle ate with the same intensity. They devoured the small carcass in minutes, then both licked their fingers until every drop of juice was consumed. Jared groaned with pleasure, his stomach satisfied for the first time since he'd left Edmonton.

"*Kinanâskomitin*," Kyle said. The warrior nodded.

"Did you say thank you? Tell him thanks from me, too." Jared took a drink from their shared canteen. He eyed the pile of bones, wishing there was more.

Kyle broke a bone and handed half to Jared. "Suck on it. The marrow is good."

Jared rolled the bone between his finger and thumb. "I feel like such a freaking savage."

Kyle's eyes narrowed to slits. He withdrew the bone from his mouth and pressed his lips together.

The double meaning of what he'd said hit Jared. "Oh man, Kyle, I didn't mean it like that. I was so hungry you could've given me a hunk of raw meat and I would've eaten it. It surprised me how...how obsessed I became about food when I couldn't eat. I tore into that meat like a starving dog. It's...kind of embarrassing."

The anger drained from Kyle's expression. "You've never been hungry before?"

"Not like this." Jared sniffed the bone, which smelled vaguely like stew. "Have you?"

"Before I moved in with Kokum and Moshum, yeah." He said it matter-of-factly, like it was no big deal.

Jared wondered about being young and hungry, expecting someone to provide supper and not getting anything. He sucked on the bone for a moment. "What I said earlier, about your people and stuff, I'm sorry, okay? I was...trying to piss you off. Wow. It worked great. The stupid thing is,

I didn't even realize how it sounded until you said it back to me. But you're right. I know nothing about what you, or any First Nations people, have gone through." He glanced askance at the warrior, who watched but seemed content to stay silent. Jared dropped the empty bone beside the discard pile and picked up another. It was harder to break than he expected. He handed half to Kyle. "What you said about my friends did hit home. Some of them are always eager for me to pay, and they do let me get my way. I thought it was because they liked me. Now I'm not sure."

"Face it, you're a rich, shallow jerk."

It was said so mildly that Jared smiled. "As shallow as that stream we waded."

Kyle laughed, a deep guffaw. The warrior smiled at him, and Jared felt a twinge of jealousy. He was the outsider here. He shifted uncomfortably. The backs of his shoes dug into his heels. He hissed, gingerly pulled off one shoe, then the other. Kyle and the warrior watched. Jared frowned. "What?"

"Do you always wear your shoes so loose?" Kyle asked.

"I guess so."

"You've got blisters, right? That's why."

"Wish you'd told me that two days ago." Jared lifted his foot and winced at the bloody spot, black on his beige sock in the dim light of the dying fire.

"You wouldn't have listened. Take your socks off. I have a few bandages in my pack."

"Guess I should've mentioned the pain earlier." Jared bit his lip and peeled the sock off. The blister had broken and was a raw bleeding mess. The other heel was the same.

"Yeah. You should've. We were both rattled after meeting that bear. Me, I've never done anything like that. I don't know if I could've fired the rifle fast enough if it had decided to charge. After it left I would've stopped if you'd said you had blisters."

Jared stretched out on his side and tried not to wince when Kyle dabbed the broken blisters with something antiseptic that stung like crazy. His head was near the warrior's knee. The stench of wolverine almost overwhelmed him again. It seemed to roll off this silent man. He must be friendly with the creature they'd seen. Why not, if this was a spirit world?

"Do you think that bear understood you? It looked like it did."

Bandages applied, Kyle gave him a long, skeptical look, shook his head, then tossed a pair of white sports socks to him. "Put these on. They're thicker than yours. And when you put your shoes back on, cinch them tight."

"Thanks. Why do you have extra socks?"

"In case my feet get wet."

"But they must be, after wading the stream."

"I'll take off my boots and dry the socks I'm wearing." He unlaced his hiking boots.

Jared sat up, glad to get away from the ripe smell of the warrior and put on the dry socks. He sighed with satisfaction and nodded at the man. "Who is he? Why doesn't he talk?"

"Maybe he doesn't want to." Kyle said a few words to the warrior in Cree. Jared didn't catch any of it, but when the warrior replied, Kyle's eyes widened and he ducked his head.

He held his knees in a white-knuckle grip. The warrior, face like a craggy mountainside, continued to speak. The fire gave his brown skin a golden cast; his dark eyes reflected the flames. The unfamiliar words ebbed and flowed around Jared like a warm ocean current. Words blended into sing-song cadence.

He was telling a story, Jared realized. Kyle's face reflected the puzzlement Jared felt curving his own brow. The man lifted his hands toward the roof, his voice rising with the smoke. Then his hands and voice both dropped and his whisper brushed over Jared. Goosebumps freckled his arms and neck.

During a pause, Jared said, "Are you understanding any of this, Kyle?"

The question earned him a glare from the warrior that increased his goosebump collection. Apparently it wasn't cool to interrupt. Kyle shook his head. "Only words here and there."

The warrior turned to Kyle. "*Kinisitohten?*"

Kyle looked uncomfortable. "*Namoya.*"

That had to mean *no*. The only word Jared caught in the next question the warrior asked was *néhiyawak*—the name for Cree that Kyle had used earlier. The question had to be hurtful because Kyle looked stricken. He gave a slow nod. "*Êhê.*" His shoulders rose and he added in a whisper, "I only know a little Cree. I wish I knew more..."

The warrior began to berate him, words thudding like a driving drum beat. Kyle started to hunch over, a turtle withdrawing into a shell, but then he straightened, lifted his chin and stared at the warrior. The tirade stopped abruptly. He looked at Jared and motioned toward Kyle. "*Sohkitehew*."

Kyle's features relaxed. He obviously understood that, and when Jared asked for a translation, Kyle avoided Jared's gaze and his cheeks seemed to darken. "He said I have a brave heart."

Jared nodded to the warrior in agreement and received a nod in return. He asked Kyle, "So what did you understand of what he said?"

"I'm pretty sure he was telling a story I've heard some elders tell, about how *Kisemanito*, the Great Spirit, made our people."

"And?"

Kyle stared. "Do you really want to know?"

Jared paused, then smiled as he realized he *did* want to hear the story. "Please tell me?"

"Okay, but the one I heard might be a bit different from the one he just told." Jared shrugged and waited. Kyle stared into the fire for a moment, then began speaking. "Short version. *Kisemanito* made the land and water, but felt something was missing. So he made animals, birds, fish, and insects. He was happy that all was in balance. After many moons, the animals cried out that they had no purpose. He thought a lot, then gave them a weaker creature to take care of—that was us. The animals cared for people, taught them how to survive." Kyle peered at the man, then at Jared. "If I was catching enough of what he was saying, that's where he stopped. The story I've heard goes longer, how people became greedy and started killing animals, and how *Kise-manito* took away the animals' power of speech and made them afraid of people to keep them safe, and how he created spirit animals to act as guides."

"We could use one of those."

"Maybe. But at least he's here."

Was that good or bad? Jared studied the man, who watched their exchange with interest. His thoughts veered to another man. "We've been gone, what, two days?"

"This is the third night," Kyle replied.

"Do you think the pilot's okay?" Kyle gave him a quizzical look and Jared added, "I mean, is it possible that help came and he was rescued even if we weren't?"

A slow smile spread across Kyle's face. "*Moniyaw*, you just thought about someone other than yourself."

"Don't be a smart ass. It happens."

"Not often, I bet."

Jared clamped his mouth shut, sorry he'd bothered to say anything.

"What? You're gonna pout? You, you're as moody as my girl cousins."

"Shut up."

Kyle gave him a measured look, shook his head and arranged his boots on their sides by the dying fire. He pulled back the tongues to expose the interior to the heat. The warrior reached over and ran a finger along one sole, his curiosity obvious. He rubbed a lace between his finger and thumb.

It reminded Jared of earlier. "Why did you look so upset when you first talked to him?"

Head down, Kyle peeled off his socks, arranged them on the rock that had held the roasted critter, then shifted his feet close to the fire. Settled into stillness, he stared into the glowing embers.

"Aren't you going to answer? Did you find out who he is?"

"Later."

"Tell me."

Kyle's glare said, *Not. Now.*

Not in front of the warrior. Maybe Kyle didn't want another telling off. Jared studied him from the corner of his eye. The man remained cross-legged, hands cupped on knees. He was ignoring them now, gaze distant, chin tilted slightly up. As if listening. A stillness, vast as a becalmed ocean, filled the room, made Jared reluctant to move, even though his backside was numbing. Kyle was equally motionless.

Jared's stomach twisted into a sour knot. He tasted acid. Swallowed, but still didn't move. He couldn't bring himself to break the silence.

A single flame flared up on the charred wood, danced in one spot, then evaporated into smoke. Embers pulsed. Slower. Slower. Jared's eyelids drooped.

The warrior exploded up and over the fire. Jared and Kyle both fell back, startled. The man knelt, spoke to Kyle, who shrugged. Frown in place, he pointed at them and tugged his ears.

"Listen." Kyle nodded. Jared leaned forward.

The man pantomimed the shape of a ball and cupped his hand as if holding it. He repeated the motion and cupped his other hand. He pointed at his first hand, then himself. Then he pointed at his second hand and at the boys. He eyed them expectantly, holding his cupped hands out toward them.

"What is this, charades? Um, ball?" Jared suggested.

"Orb? Globe?" Kyle added.

"Earth?" Jared shrugged.

"Yes." Kyle pointed at the hand nearest him. "World. *Askîy.*"

The warrior nodded, repeated the word as he motioned between his left hand and himself, and repeated it again as he motioned between the boys and his right hand.

"I get it," Jared said. "The left hand holds his world and the right hand holds ours."

Kyle nodded. That earned a grim smile from the man. "*Kinisitohten?*"

"We understand." Kyle nodded more boldly.

The warrior mimed a rod between his two hands.

"A connection," Kyle suggested. Jared agreed. Understanding must have shown because the man gave a single terse nod. He tugged his ears again.

"This part must be important," Jared said.

The warrior pointed at each of them then made a breaking motion. He raised and lowered his cupped hands out of synch. He paused, looking for understanding.

"Seriously?" Jared sighed. "What's that supposed to mean?"

After going through the series of motions two more times, the man rested his hands on his thighs and waited, but his gaze seemed to intensify, to demand they get his message.

"Let's break it down," Kyle said, and he mimicked the warrior's movements as he spoke. "He showed us that there are two worlds, his and ours. Then he motioned that the worlds are connected."

"Right." Jared swallowed a lump as the curtain started to lift. "And he pointed at us just before he snapped an invisible twig and did the seesaw thing."

Their gazes met. Jared knew he likely looked as worried as Kyle did. He whispered, "The guy can't mean that we messed up the connection between our worlds, can he?"

"I think he does. The worlds are out of balance." Kyle bit his lip, copied the seesaw motion, and searched the warrior's grave face. He touched his own chest and Jared's arm, then motioned breaking. "*Pîkona?* We broke it?" The warrior nodded. Kyle shrugged, turning up his hands in a helpless gesture.

Anger twisted the man's face into a fierce mask. He clenched his hands, held out his fists and jerked them toward each other, then made a circular motion. He repeated it and pointed at them.

"What does he want us to do?" Jared asked, though he had a growing suspicion.

"He showed us breaking the connection." Kyle rubbed the back of his neck. "The fists were like jamming two things together."

"The broken connection."

"Yeah. And that last motion was running? Circling?"

The memory of Kyle wrapping the pilot's head came to mind, his hand circling the bloodied scalp. Dread simmered in Jared's gut. "He was wrapping. We're supposed to fix the connection. How are we supposed to freaking do that?"

Kyle gave him a puzzled glance. He motioned to the warrior and them, then made the fixing and wrapping motions.

"*Namoya!*" the warrior snapped. He jabbed his finger toward them, repeated the repair actions, then crossed his arms. As if to say the conversation was over.

Jared withered under the man's glare. He couldn't be serious. It was insane. They had no special powers. They couldn't fix a rift between worlds. Inside, dread lurched from bubbling to swirling. Losing his supper became a real possibility. Kyle rubbed his mouth; he also looked tinged with green. And deeply worried.

The warrior's attention shifted. He peered over his shoulder for a moment. Countenance grim, he pointed at Jared, then Kyle. "*Kisata. Kisata.*" He leaned toward Kyle, apparently asking him if he understood, continuing when Kyle nodded. His voice dropped too low for Jared to hear. Then the warrior slipped into the night.

A tremor leaked into Jared's words. "W-what did he say?"

"We have to stay here. *Kisata.* Until early morning, *wapan.* I think he said to sleep."

"Like I can to do that after he ordered us to fix the world. Sure, dude, right after I take out the trash." Jared's attempted mockery felt hollow. "Now can you tell me who he is?"

Kyle dropped his voice low. "*Wesakechak.*" He checked his socks, turned them over with jerky motions, as if his limbs weren't quite obeying his brain. His throat convulsed. "In Cree legends, *Wesakechak* is a trickster."

It almost sounded like Kyle had said Whiskey Jack, the gray bird that had hassled them on the walk up the hill. But not quite. We-sak-e-chak. Jared shifted closer. "A trickster? And I suppose you expect us to trust this guy?"

"Us, we might have to. He...said something else."

"You just said he's a known con man. What could he say that would make you want to trust him? That's crazy. If he said stay, we should go." When Kyle's worried look deepened, Jared relented. "Okay. What else did he say?"

"He said that he's coming."

"He? He who?"

"You know who."

The word hung between them.

Wîhtiko.

13

Trickster

You know who. The phrase bounced around in Jared's brain, dislodging panic. He blurted, "We need to run."

"*Wesakechak* said to stay. If nothing else, you have to trust this: in our stories, he has never helped *Wîhtiko*." Kyle whispered the monster's name so quietly Jared felt more than heard the word. "In our stories he usually helps people."

"But not always."

Kyle's silence seemed like agreement.

Outside, the sounds of shuffling drew their attention. Barely more than a shadow in the light of the fading embers, Kyle crept to the door and peered out. Another sound drew Jared forward. It sounded like...running water.

Kyle held the flap closed and leaned against the wall of poles, the uncertainty of his wrinkled forehead visible even in the near darkness.

"Wha—" Jared's question was cut short by the spray of water on the outside of the leather door. "Is he...?"

"Pissing on the door. Yeah. And he pissed on the ground in front of the door, too."

"That's disgusting."

The smell that had grossed out Jared when they first entered the moss house came back in a vile wave. Jared clamped his hand over his mouth to stop from barfing. His eyes watered.

Moonlight filtered in through the hut's smoke hole, grew brighter, and transformed the interior from black into shades of gray. The only spot of color was the diminishing red eye of the fire's remains.

The stream of urine stopped, but the stink lingered.

"Why would he *do* that?" Jared whispered. He crawled over to where Kyle once again cracked open the leather flap. On his stomach, Jared cupped his hand over nose and mouth and nudged the corner of the flap aside so he could see out.

The warrior was gone. The moonlight gave the village a ghostly silver sheen and threw shadows black enough to swallow a man. Jared grew more certain this warrior was the same guy he'd seen the previous night. There had been a moment before the man had moved last night, when he'd seemed to define stillness, as if he never moved more than necessary. He'd been the same way tonight. The dog stink added to his certainty. If it *was* him, then he had lured *Wîhtiko* away. So if he had helped them last night, then maybe he could be trusted. It wasn't like they had a lot of choices in this unpopulated wilderness.

A trickster, Kyle had said. Jared had once done a report for school on the Norse gods. That lore had a trickster named Loki who was nearly always bad news. Maybe Cree tricksters were different. Jared was about to ask Kyle when he noticed movement beyond the village, by the stream he and Kyle had waded across earlier.

"Did you see that?" he whispered.

"Yeah. Shh." The voice came from above him.

A cloud's shadow scudded across the whole village. Everything became black on black. The putrid smell of urine and wet dog seemed stronger in the darkness, smothering. Jared wanted to tear out of the moss house, to run and not stop running until he found daylight. All that anchored him was the knee touching his shoulder and the sound of Kyle's measured breathing above him. He knew he should back away from the door flap, that it would probably be easier to stay calm if he wasn't looking outside. But the thought of not knowing what was going on when his life was at stake was way worse than leaving his gifts unopened under the Christmas tree. He'd always opened one end to peek inside then taped them closed. Knowledge was power. The only power he had in this place.

Moonlight skated back, gliding over the marsh, up and over the moss houses on the left. Then, as if a switch had been thrown, the village lay stark and silver before them.

Wîhtiko stood by the farthest house, arms hanging slack. It turned its head back and forth, then swung to the house on its right, lunged toward the doorway and stuck its head inside, hands clamped on the doorframe. Even at this distance its rasping breaths were audible. *Hiss. Heh. Hiss. Heh.*

It lurched back onto the pathway. Instead of checking the house across the path, it lumbered toward the second house on its right. Paused near the doorway. Inhaled loudly. And again. The sound quivered over Jared's skin. His mouth dried out.

It smelled their trail. And they were in a house with only one exit. Jared tried to warn Kyle, but could only produce a quiet squeak. Under his breath, Kyle shushed him.

Wîhtiko shuffled to the third house on its right. Jared's stomach clenched so tightly he had to swallow bile. *It's only checking the houses I went into. It smells me.*

The monster forced its way through the small doorway. Thudding, crashing. Growling. It pitched out of the third house, wheeled around, and around, then faced their hiding place. It flung its head back and screamed. An eerie, bone-shattering sound.

Cold wove into muscle and marrow. Encased Jared in frozen terror. He couldn't look away. Couldn't twitch a finger. Could barely remember to breathe. Kyle's labored wheezing echoed what Jared felt. That scream had paralyzed them.

Wîhtiko took two steps forward and stopped, so close Jared could see its caved cheeks and tattered lips, bits of flesh hanging down, sucking in and out of its mouth with each breath. Its nose was a torn hole. Its clothing was shredded, held together by strands of leather. The shirt's torn-away front revealed its cadaverous body, a skeleton with skin that was gray in the moonlight. It didn't seem to have shrunk since devouring that deer.

It raised its arms high, hands outstretched. Something dark streaked down from its oddly stubby fingers. Blood? It licked one hand's mutilated fingers, shot the hand back into the air and screamed again, louder, fiercer.

Like frost creeping across a window, ice crackled over Jared's skin. Cold like he'd never felt seeped inside, a tractor beam holding him motionless. His breath rattled in his lungs. Air barely seeped down his throat.

Wîhtiko lowered its arms. Sniffed loudly. Turned its head. Jared struggled to close his eyes so it wouldn't see them reflecting in the moonlight, but even his eyelids were frozen. His eyes ached as they dried out.

Sniff. A half-step forward. *Sniff.*

The skeletal face turned toward their shelter. Its mouth opened, a dark and rotting cave.

And this, thought Jared, *is how it ends. Wîhtiko can track my smell because I don't belong in this world. And Kyle will die because he tried to help me.*

14

Pissing Contest

Wîhtiko **exhaled,** sniffed and snorted. Its finger stubs curled inward. It flung itself to the right and stumbled noisily around the moss house, snarling and grating its teeth. It stopped in front of the doorway, its back to the covered opening. Sniffing.

Jared still couldn't move. Why weren't they dead? It could smell his trail, so what was stopping it? Had the warrior cast some kind of spell? Was he magical?

A booming voice rolled out from the far end of the village. "*Wîhtiko!*" The warrior yelled at the monster in Cree. The net of fear released Jared, like handcuffs springing open. He rolled away from the door flap, silently struggling to regain his breath.

Kyle was still crouched by his viewing crack. He sagged down with a sigh, also released. He continued to watch outside, and muffled a sound of surprise. Jared wanted to ask what was happening, but was afraid to make a sound. Through the ground, he felt the vibrations of heavy footsteps fading away.

Kyle fell away from the doorway, scuttled backwards and collapsed by the fire. Even mostly hidden by darkness, his limbs shook visibly. Jared realized he too was shaking.

"Is it gone?" His voice was sandpaper rough.

"Yes." Kyle groaned. "*Wesakechak* saved us with his piss."

Did that even make sense? Jared felt too drained to figure it out. "How?"

"It killed our scent."

Jared clutched his knees to his chest. "You mean *my* scent. You saw how it only went in the houses I'd checked out."

No response. Jared pressed his forehead to his knees. He'd wanted Kyle to deny what he'd seen. Every ounce of him quaked. *Wihtiko* wasn't hunting *them*; it was hunting *him*. He fought rising panic, refused to unlock his limbs and let them flail like they wanted. "W-why?"

"Why is it chasing you?" Jared managed a tiny nod that Kyle couldn't have seen, but he answered as if he had. "Me, I'm guessing that it smells your city stink. My stink, it's from the bush. But you, you carry the smell of pollution and electric stuff. And of that blue jacket."

"So it's n-not because I'm wh-wh--"

"White? Doubt it. I'm betting we're both just meat to it. Can't imagine our skin color makes our meat taste different."

"That's disgusting," Jared whispered.

Kyle snorted. "Though, now that I think about it, I do hang around lots of campfires in the summer. Maybe that gives me a smoked flavor. Maybe it doesn't like smoked—"

"Shut up." Anger seized Jared's muscles, tightened them. The shaking stopped. "This isn't a joke. How can you joke about this?" He realized how close he was to the door flap, and half crawled, half scrambled toward the back of the hut.

Reason #9: he laughs at things that aren't at all funny.

The moon had migrated; pale light now painted half of three logs. He settled under the bar of illumination and glared in the direction of Kyle's shadowed form. "This is completely *un*funny. You're twisted."

"Who said I was joking?" Kyle shifted, too, and rustled around one pile of spruce boughs. "Me, I'm guessing. It might think like that."

"Well, I don't want to hear your guesses. I don't want to know anything about how a monster like that thinks."

"Wrong answer, *Moniyaw*. If we want to escape it, we've got to learn how it thinks. Like tracking an animal. Know how it thinks and you can figure out where to look for it if you lose its trail. Only here, the animal is tracking us and we need to figure out how to make it lose *our* trail."

"You make it sound like a game."

"Yeah. Lots of things can be games. If it helps, think of this as a, a game of chess. Only in this case our 'king' is our lives. Checkmate equals, well..." Kyle made a squelching noise.

Irritation bubbled up. "Chess again? What do you know about playing chess?"

"What does that mean?"

"You're. You're—"

"Too dumb? The Cree boy is too dumb?"

Jared pressed his lips together and sniffed. "I didn't mean it like that. I'm just surprised you know anything about chess. My dad made me learn, said it was the 'game of kings' and modern kings are heads of corporations, so it was a game I should know. I didn't think someone who lived—"

"On a reserve?"

"Yes. That anyone, um...uneducated would bother to..." Jared sighed. It was coming out all wrong.

"I should've known that deep well of stupid would over-flow again."

Jared cringed. It had sounded stupid. More rustling. Then the sound of something flop-flopping. Jared could barely see Kyle doing something by his pile of branches. Then his form flatted into the shadows. He was going to bed, Jared realized.

When he was still again, Kyle said, "My moshum loves chess, loves to outfox his opponent. He never finished school, but no one can beat him so he has to play online. And I bet your father never told you the game came from India. It wasn't invented by whites. Lots of things weren't. You're just good at stealing things."

"I know you're not dumb, Kyle. Cut me some slack. I'm freaked out enough without you piling historical race stuff on me. All I know is that we're in a colossal mess and it's my fault, but not because I'm white or rich. If it helps, I'm sorry that I am."

"Mostly, you're stupid."

Reason #10: he enjoys calling me stupid.

"Back off, jerk. Yes, I made a bad decision going up that hill. But I'm not stupid. I get good marks in school. High seventies, low eighties."

"So? I told you Kokum makes sure I do good in school. My average in grade ten was eighty-six percent. But that schooling isn't going to help us out here."

"I have street smarts, too."

"Doubt it. You might know which streets to avoid at night, but if someone pulls a knife and demands your money? If you're in an alley in the rough part of town and you have to stay there all night, can you tell me you'd have a clue what to do?"

Jared released a slow breath. "Other than call for help on my cell? No."

"So here we are in the bush, the place where I spend my summers and lots of weekends, being chased by a something that wants to eat us, and you argue with me, and you insist you're better than me. Does it make you feel good about yourself to think you're better?"

Jared wanted to argue, but there was too much truth in Kyle's words. He *had* thought of himself as better. But the last dregs of his superiority had drained into that stream when he'd been cowering on the rocks and Kyle had been standing up to a bear. A freaking bear! He was everything Kyle said: puny, mostly helpless, and not very nice about it.

Unfortunately, his old thoughts hadn't quite adjusted to this new point of view. And they popped out at inconvenient times, like a bad habit that you can't shake. Maybe he did have a deep well of stupid. The question was, how could he at least seal it off so nothing got out? "Tell me what to do."

"Grow a pair of ears." A grunt escaped as Kyle's black silhouette rolled over. "And go to sleep."

"S-sleep?"

"Yeah. Roll out the moose hide beside your bed and wrap up in it. Close your eyes. You know the drill. Same in the bush as in the city." Another snort. "Except for the moose hide."

"But, what if *Wîh*—what if it comes back?"

"*Wesakechak* said we should stay 'til morning. We'll be safe until then."

"How can you know?"

"I don't, but I'm choosing to trust him. Are you gonna trust me?"

Jared's body was becoming lead. If he didn't lie down soon, he'd fall asleep sitting up. "Yes. I'm going to trust you. And…I'll work on the ear thing."

A throat clearing seemed to say, *I'll hold you to that.* In moments Jared was cocooned in moose hide. To his right, Kyle began to snore quietly.

Outside, a dry twig snapped. Jared's eyes bulged as he stared at the darkened doorway. Tired as he was, he suddenly knew he'd never sleep. His heart thudded as he waited for the flimsy door to be flung aside.

15

Morning

Jared broke the surface of sleep, choking as if he'd been held under water too long. He bolted upright and thumped his head on the slanted wall of the moss house. His last thoughts had been about swimming a leisurely front crawl. Stroke, stroke, stroke, breathe. Stroke, stroke, stroke, breathe.

His head sagged forward as he tried to remember what had woken him, but his dreams remained formless. They left a taste, though, a taste of dread.

He licked his lips, rubbed at his front teeth with his finger. He hadn't brushed his teeth for days, and he was pretty sure the moss stuck onto this house had migrated and taken up permanent residence on his molars. "I feel gross."

Kyle propped himself onto his elbow. The moose hide fell off his shoulder. "You look it, too. Thought it the first time I saw you." He grinned.

A smile twitched at one corner of Jared's mouth. "You're a craptastic liar."

Kyle flung the hide the rest of the way off, twisted up to sit cross-legged on the moose hide. "Which part of your grossness did you finally notice?"

Jared rolled his eyes. "My breath."

"Yeah, I can smell it from here."

Jared huffed into his cupped palm and smelled. It wasn't *that* bad. He noticed Kyle's shoulders shaking slightly. "Funny. Any chance you have an extra toothbrush in that pack?"

"Why would I even have one?"

"You had extra socks."

"Yeah, in case my feet got wet. In the bush wet feet are bad news. I wasn't expecting to be gone even one night."

"So no toothbrush."

Kyle tugged on his boots, tied them, and folded his moose hide blanket. "Could be good. Such bad breath, it might scare *Wîhtiko* away, knock it over, or gas it."

Jared released a sigh. He followed Kyle's lead and folded his bedding, such as it was.

"Okay, so maybe that wasn't funny," Kyle admitted. "You go piss and I'll find a willow."

"For what?"

"To brush your teeth like a real outdoorsman."

"Sure. Just call me Mr. Outback."

"Thought you said your last name was Fredrickson or something."

Kyle smiled again. Jared rubbed his neck. "I don't know why you're so freaking cheerful this morning, but fine. Cleaning my teeth with willow leaves sounds like a real blast."

"A good night's sleep is magic." Kyle picked up the canteen, pushed past the door flap, and left a wake of silence behind.

Jared pulled on his sneakers, careful to tie them as snugly as he could, like Kyle had instructed. He paused by the door-frame, gripped it tightly until he convinced himself that it was safe to go out. Finally he stepped onto the welcome mat of spruce boughs and stopped, but only until he remembered that *Wesakechak* had urinated on these branches to kill their scent. Two strides took him away from the entrance, still thick with the stench of urine and wolverine. Had *Wesake-chak* gotten his four-legged friend to roll around out here or something? Had the animal rubbed up against him? Was that why he stank? Why the whole interior stank?

That stench had kept them alive, but the inside of his nose felt like it had been burned raw with a blow-torch. Jared scanned the village; he couldn't see Kyle until he moved to check behind *Wesakechak's* moss house. Kyle was skirting the marsh, heading toward a clump of bushes with silvery leaves.

The marsh reflected a sky that was still pinkish near the horizon. Jared never got up at dawn, unless it was for an early swim practice. He stretched, rubbed his lower arms against the chill and circled behind the nearest house close to the trees. He started forward, intending to step behind a tree for privacy, but couldn't bring himself to leave the village's clearing and the sense of security it gave him. He urinated onto the base of the tree he'd stopped in front of, closed his eyes and remembered the hollow sound of *Wesakechak* urinating on the door flap. He shuddered, shook himself dry. His fingers fumbled with the button flap and he was still doing up the top button when he spun and rushed back to the "street" between the two rows of houses.

Jared crouched a yard from the spruce boughs fronting *Wesakechak's* doorway. He couldn't stop scanning the edges of the village and the far shore of the marsh. From reeds along the water, a bird began chirping a distinctive tune. He knew now that a bird wouldn't chirp if a monster was nearby. Still his gaze kept darting to where the stream entered the marsh, the place where *Wîhtiko* had appeared.

Movement. Jared sprang up. He was poised on the balls of his feet, ready to flee, when Kyle stepped out of the trees. He had to have circled around through the forest. He crouched by the stream for a few moments, his back to Jared, then stood, canteen in hand. He started toward the village, giving a brief wave when he noticed Jared.

His calmness was an anchor. Here he was, in the midst of a nightmare, and he was telling jokes—really bad jokes, but at least they were jokes—and doing what needed to be done without complaint. He was, Jared realized, a really likeable guy. Sure he'd gotten pissed off a few times, but it was usually with reason. He didn't deserve to be here working to save some pathetic city boy's skin.

Pathetic city boy. PCB. Weren't real PCBs some kind of toxic chemicals?

Jared shoved his hand in his pocket, searching for his phone. Not there. Alarmed, he patted his pockets, turned up his dead iPod and its earbuds, rubbed the iPod as he remembered smashing his phone. He stuck in one earbud and turned on his music. Nothing, not even static. Lips compressed, he shoved the dead device back into its pocket. Everything he usually used or depended on was useless.

Kyle strode down the beaten path and when he reached Jared he handed over the canteen. Jared took a long drink, handed it back, and wiped his mouth with the back of his hand. He nodded his thanks.

"Why'd you go to the stream through the trees?"

"Never hurts to scout. Can't tell what time of year it is here, but I think it's later in the summer than back in our world, so I was hoping to find some berries."

"Did you?"

"No. Found some mint, though." Kyle emptied one pocket of his camouflage jacket, producing some twigs and separate leaves. He handed over a twig. "Your willow toothbrush."

Jared curled his lip as he examined it. "A stick? I thought you were bringing willow leaves."

"The leaves, they're good for boiling up willow tea. Nature's Tylenol. See how I cut the twig ends diagonally, leaving more interior exposed? You rub that against your teeth, same as a toothbrush. It works pretty good. Then you chew a few mint leaves for minty fresh breath."

He extended his hand, palm up. The small jagged-edged leaves were dark green and eye-shaped, almost fuzzy looking. Jared took one and sniffed.

"Crush it if you want to smell."

Jared did and was rewarded with a whiff of mint. Pressure gathered behind his eyes. Kyle had done nothing but help him, was still helping him, and was always willing to teach him.

Reason #11 we couldn't be friends: why would a nice guy want to be friends with a PCB?

Twirling the willow twig in his fingers, he kept his head down, and took a deep breath before he spoke. "I think you should leave." He exhaled slowly. Being alone was the last thing he wanted. But it was the right thing. Why did the right thing feel so rock-bottom awful?

"What?"

"Leave. You should leave. I can stay in *Wesakechak's* house where my scent is covered up. You'll have a better chance of finding a way home without me slowing you down."

"Yeah?" Kyle struck Jared's shoulder with the heel of his hand. "And what about you?"

Jared shrugged but didn't look up. He had no answer. Hadn't thought past the first step. "I'll...figure something out."

"Two brains are better than one for figuring."

"But if *Wîhtiko* smells *me*, Kyle, you can get away."

"To do what? Go home and tell Kokum that I left you to die?"

"I'm not going to, to—"

"But you are. Don't you get it?" Kyle hit his shoulder again and he staggered back a step. "*Moniyaw*, you don't know how to find food, how to live. You'll shrivel up and starve to death in this moss house, or you'll go into the forest where *Wîhtiko* will hunt you down."

"Okay." Jared nodded, kept nodding. "We've established I'm useless. But I'm more than that, Kyle. I'm toxic! That monster can smell me." Now Jared shoved Kyle, but it only made him slide his foot back half a step or less. "Remember our argument before the bear? You said that if it came to that, you didn't think you'd give your life to save mine. Well, I don't want you to. I want you to get away."

Kyle's features puckered into something between confused and surprised. "You're doing it again."

"What?"

"Thinking of someone else."

Jared clenched his fists and resisted the urge to hit Kyle. The willow twig dug into his palm. "It probably won't happen again, so take advantage of it."

Kyle shrugged. "Don't want to."

Jared's energy drained and he sank to his knees. "Please. This is new for me, this whole thinking about someone else thing. If something happens to you what am I supposed to do? I-I don't want to live with the guilt of knowing you could've gotten away."

Kyle squatted beside him. "And I don't want to live with the guilt of leaving you to die. Been there. Once was enough."

"What does *that* mean?"

Kyle folded down to sit cross-legged. He absently rubbed his twig over his teeth and frowned at nothing, or maybe at memories. Jared was about to urge him to talk when he spoke. "I was eight. Dad and me, we were headed to the city to find an apartment he could rent while he went to technical school for an apprenticeship thing. He was going to be a plumber." He scrubbed the fronts of his teeth with the twig for a moment. "It was a drunk driving accident." He jabbed the twig at Jared. "Don't even think that Dad was the drunk."

Jared leaned away from the stick. "I didn't say anything."

The anger pursing Kyle's mouth eased. "Yeah. Sorry. I guess I am a little touchy about that with you."

A little? Instead of commenting, which was tempting (and probably why Kyle was touchy, because Jared couldn't seem to *not* comment), Jared merely gave a nod and tried rubbing the willow stick on his front teeth. It left a bitter taste in his mouth.

Kyle crushed his mint leaves and inhaled deeply, as if he wanted to erase the stink of his memories. "It was a white lady, middle-aged and loaded. She flew off a side road in a streak of silver. Slammed into our old pickup. Hit the driver's door. Other than a real sore neck and some bruises, I was mostly okay because Dad was strict about seatbelts. Dad, he probably died right away, but when I couldn't wake him up I thought that if I went for help, a doctor would know how to make him better. So I left him. Ran to a farm down the road. The old guy there, he almost chased me away, but I was pointing and there was smoke rising from the accident, so he finally believed me and called for help. The lady, she was fine except for a broken nose from her airbag."

"That sucks."

"No kidding, right? Kokum, she said I had survivor's guilt. She's a nurse so I guess she knows. All I know is that I still wake up once in a while with the sound of screaming metal in my ears."

"Leaving me here isn't the same."

"How do you figure?"

"Because if you stay we might both die, and what good is that? Isn't it better if one of us gets out of this?"

"Noble doesn't suit you, *Moniyaw*."

"Don't you think I know that? It's not the same but I lost my dad, too. By divorce. Except I kind of ended up losing both parents." Jared kept his head down, twirled the stick between finger and thumb. "I thought we were happy. Or, not unhappy, except when Dad was pissed off. Though we never really did anything together. Now they both feel guilty, I guess, but what happens is that neither one seems to want to deal with me. Mom always gets my stepdad to talk to me. Dad only takes me in the summer because that was the court deal. But they're both good at shoving guilt money at me. So I've learned to play that, soak both of them as much as I can." Jared gave a terse half laugh. "Which, listening to myself, makes me a real jerk. And you know what? All your talk about your kokum? You have someone in your family you care about that much, someone you respect that much. I hate it. Which makes me a bigger jerk."

"Hardly worth saving."

"Exactly."

"But hey, you've thought about someone else twice in less than twelve hours. So maybe you *are* worth saving."

"Now who's being freaking noble?"

"But that's my right. I'm the noble savage." Jared shot his head up, eyes wide, to see Kyle smiling. "You ever call me that, though, I'll crush you."

Before he could reply, Jared's stomach rumbled loudly.

Kyle laughed. "Unless your gut eats you from the inside out first."

Jared's shoulders slumped as the tension eased. "I think it's happening already. Where's the nearest takeout?"

"A world away."

"I figured you'd say that. I'm really not going to convince you to leave, am I?"

"Not without you. But we should both go. *Wesakechak,* he said to stay until morning, not longer." He stood. "Come on. Let's test those bandages of yours." He disappeared into the moss house and returned with his backpack and rifle. And a smile.

It was stupid. They were in a spirit world where a monster wanted to eat them. Or maybe just him. But still Jared smiled back. Whatever came, he didn't have to face it alone. He had to bite back a chuckle. Laughing was more ridiculous than smiling, but his relief was like a blast of fresh air blowing away the stink clinging to *Wesakechak's* house.

Kyle clasped his outstretched hand and yanked him to his feet. "Let's make tracks."

"Isn't the point to avoid leaving tracks so we're harder to follow?"

Kyle tilted his head and squinted one eye. "You really don't know that that means to get moving?" When Jared shrugged, Kyle shook his head. "You and me, we live in different worlds."

Jared sighed. "Sure wish we were in a different world right now."

"Wishing won't get us anywhere." He handed Jared a finger-length piece of dried meat. "Last of the pemmican. Take small bites and chew slowly. Let's walk."

They headed out of the village on a trail that kept to the edge of the marsh. Jared nibbled the pemmican and mosquitoes nibbled him. He continually swatted at the pests. When he commented on it, Kyle noted that they laid eggs in still water; even in a dry year a marsh was a great mosquito breeding ground.

When they reached the end of the watery clearing, Kyle paused to scan the area. The trail, so beaten that even Jared could spot it, moved into the forest and angled up a small hill. It reminded Jared of a narrow alley wedged between tall buildings. Mosquitoes or not, he liked the openness of the marsh. The few trees in the water were gray skeletons, narrow and sparse, some broken off like vandalized street signs. The far end of the marsh was more than a city block away, and Jared liked seeing that far, especially knowing a creature that could smell him was out there.

Jared squinted over swaying treetops toward the hill, somehow menacing even at this distance, like a thundercloud about to open up. He lifted the stick he was still carrying and tried to rub it over his teeth in the same way he usually brushed them. The sour sap taste filled his mouth. He tossed the stick away. It landed with a plop in the water. He shuddered as his gaze shifted from the hill to the trees. As he wondered about their rhythmic tossing, he popped the mint leaves in his mouth and chewed.

A strong peppermint taste exploded in his mouth. He

sucked in air to weaken it a bit, then chewed some more. Kyle tapped his shoulder and pointed at the path. They started up the slope. When the leaves were mulch in his mouth, Jared wondered if he should spit or swallow. A low rumble from his gut made up his mind: he swallowed.

The path topped the small hill and followed its crest. They stopped again. Wind riffled through the trees. Branches shook, released decaying leaves, and swiped at their faces.

"Windy up here," Jared commented. He took a deep breath, enjoying that no hint of the odor from *Wesakechak's* house remained. But in its place was the smell of smoke, stronger now than he'd ever smelled it.

Kyle scowled toward the west. Between the trees Jared could see distant smoke drifting over the forest's rooftop.

"Is that where you're taking us?" Jared asked. "Can we lose *Wîhtiko* in the smoke?"

"Maybe, but it's too risky. This kind of wind can shift and trap a person who's too close, surround them by fire before they can escape."

"Then why are we heading toward it?"

"I...thought we'd find help going that way." Kyle's shoulders hunched and he stuffed his hands in his coat pockets. "Now, I don't know. Fire's coming this way. With this wind, it could come fast."

Though he faced the smoke plume, Jared could feel the presence of the hill behind him. It seemed to lie in wait, a treacherous beast you should never turn your back on. Like the monster it sheltered. Kyle seemed lost in thought as he glared at the far-off smoke. Jared faced the specter haunting his thoughts. Why was the hill so magnetic? There had to be a reason why they couldn't escape its influence.

Maybe to find out, they had to—Jared veered his thoughts away. *No freaking way.* But the idea wormed its way back. *Wesakechak* had said Kyle had a brave heart, and Kyle had said that running rarely solved the problem. Which brought him back to the one thing that made sense, the one thing he didn't want to do.

Jared attempted to inhale courage. He coughed. "Want to know what I think?"

Kyle didn't even look at him. Jared swatted a branch. "I know I'm just the city idiot here, but you could at least pretend to listen."

Hands shook free of their pockets. Kyle crossed his arms and turned to eye Jared. As if blatant scorn was better.

Jared lifted his chin. "I think we're going the wrong way." He flung his arm out and pointed west. "That fire agrees with me."

"Yeah? And where should we be going then?"

"Back to the hill."

Disbelief stamped Kyle's face.

Now that he'd said it out loud, it made complete sense. The hill was demanding their attention. Maybe it was time they listened. Maybe they needed to stop running, to return to the source of their problem and figure this out. "Hear me out before you slap me down. We arrived here because we went up the hill, right? So doesn't it make sense that we could get back to our own world somewhere on that hill? Maybe it's a trap, but just maybe *Wesakechak* or, or your kokum's prayers are keeping the hill in our minds to draw us back. We need to find out."

Kyle's frown deepened. His expression turned thoughtful.

"Say something."

Kyle unfolded his arms and slid his hands back into his pockets. He squinted in the direction of the hill and shook his head slowly.

"What? You think I'm wrong?"

"Worse than that, Jared. I think you're right."

16

A Tribe

Jared was so shocked he could barely respond. Kyle hadn't called him *Moniyaw*. He'd actually called him Jared. It was...disorienting. Almost like he was an equal.

That was a lie. When he'd first been rescued by Kyle he'd seen himself as the superior one. But in this alien environment called the wilderness, he was definitely inferior. He didn't know anything, not even what was safe to eat. His stomach growled on cue. That tiny strip of pemmican had barely touched his hunger.

"You okay?" Kyle poked his shoulder. "You're looking kind of stunned."

"You said I was right."

"Yeah. It's crazy."

A gust of wind shook the trees and sent a shiver down Jared's spine. "Speaking of crazy, about last night..." Kyle tilted his head and gave him a questioning look. Jared cleared his throat. "Was it just me, or did that scream act like some kind of freeze ray on you, too?"

"Yeah. It did." Kyle shivered visibly. "I don't remember Kokum telling us any stories about *Wîhtiko* where that happened. It's not good."

"Freaking understatement of the year."

Kyle snorted. "Scared?"

"Hell yes. Weren't you the one who said that sometimes scared is the smartest thing you can be?" Jared folded his arms against the fear that shifted and swirled along the currents like a living thing, and snaked around his throat at the mere mention of its presence.

"I didn't think you were listening."

"I'm listening now. Believe me, I'll listen to any ideas you have about how to get home."

"You said it. We have to get back to the hill."

"So we have to backtrack to the village and the stream? Retrace our steps?"

"I don't think so. We're northwest of the hill now. I think if we use the compass and game trails we can cut across country and save some distance."

Jared pulled the compass from his pocket and held it out. "It's all yours."

"No. You keep us on track. That frees me up to keep an eye on the trail and—"

"And what?"

"And anything that might be tracking us."

Jared lowered his head and studied the compass. He didn't want Kyle to see how much that statement unnerved him.

Hunger forgotten, his gut quivered. That kind of deep unease had to show on a person's face. He'd never thought of himself as a coward, had never backed down from anyone who dared to hassle him at school. But he'd always had his friends backing him up, he realized. He'd never faced anything alone. Didn't even know how.

His hand curled around the compass. His lips pressed together as an unexpected sense of determination stole over him. He wasn't alone now, either. And frankly, in this situation, he'd rather have Kyle with him than any—or all—of his friends from home. They'd be as useless as him.

He raised his face and nodded at Kyle. "Let's do this."

Kyle eyed the nearest tree, pointed in the general direction of the sun. "We need to go that way, but you'd better check."

Jared walked himself through using the compass with whispered directions. When he had southeast figured out he pointed—in the same direction Kyle had indicated a minute earlier. "How did you know which way to go?"

"You should've been a Boy Scout. At least then you'd know that moss grows thickest on the north sides of trees." Kyle started out, leaving Jared to frown at the fuzz-covered base of the tree beside him.

He caught up to Kyle. "You should have decked me."

"What are you talking about?"

"Before we went up the hill the first time. You should've knocked me out and dragged me back to the jet."

"What? And ruined your nice pretty shoes?"

Jared glanced down at his dusty, scuffed CRs. The corner

of one gold stripe had obviously hooked on something and was sticking out. "I would have hated you for ruining my shoes, but yes."

"Now you don't care?"

About shoes? Or even about his smashed iPhone? "Let's say my priorities are different now."

"You want to get home safely."

"Not quite. I want *both of us* to get home safely."

Kyle came to an abrupt halt and spun around. He eyed Jared up and down, then nodded. "Me, too. Cree people, we work together for the good of the whole tribe. We work together to survive. Spending time with *Wesakechak* last night made me realize that in this world, whether we like it or not, you and me are a tribe."

A smile tugged at Jared's lips. "A tribe of two."

A rumble quaked through his insides.

Kyle suppressed a laugh, though a smile still touched his squinting eyes. "We'd better find food soon or your stomach's growling will lead *Wîhtiko* straight to us."

They marched on in a general southeast direction, taking trails Jared could barely see until they were on them, zigging down one path then darting down another. Jared's stomach continued to rail against its empty fate, but he didn't see the point of commenting since Kyle could probably hear the rumbling.

Mid-morning, they were traversing a valley when Kyle waded off the path, through a patch of weeds, and halted beside a low bush. Jared followed gingerly, watching for stinging nettles, trying not to touch anything. He stopped by a waist-high bush with serrated leaves shaped similar to a maple leaf and clusters of bright red berries.

"Red currants. They're kind of sour to eat straight off the bush." Kyle plucked one translucent berry free and tossed it into his mouth. "But if you're hungry..."

Jared needed no invitation. He spent several minutes frantically picking the berries and gobbling them down by the handful. Berries ruptured in his mouth in micro-bursts of sourness; most he swallowed without chewing. He choked on a cluster, stems and all. Spit them out. Grabbed for more.

A hand clamped on his shoulder. "Take it easy. You're gonna get a major gut ache if you eat too many at once. Let's fill our pockets and keep moving."

Jared stopped with a handful of berries halfway to his mouth. He squashed the urge to argue and popped one berry into his mouth, closing his eyes as he bit down. His nose wrinkled at the tartness. He lifted the buckskin shirt's hem to form an open pouch and filled it. He noticed one berry squished on his sleeve. It looked like a drop of blood.

He groaned slightly as he stood. Kyle shushed him. "Listen."

Jared strained to hear whatever it was Kyle was talking about. "I don't hear anything."

"Right. We should hear at least distant birdsong. Forests aren't really quiet places."

"So...?"

"Something's made every animal and bird in this valley nervous enough to fall silent."

Pressure snaked around his chest. He tried to listen for a

sound. Any sound. All he heard was a *whoosh whoosh whoosh* filling his ears, the sound of frantically pumping blood. He licked dry lips and whispered, "We should go?"

"Quickly and quietly."

Kyle led the way, breaking into a jog when he could, slowing down for obstacles then speeding up again. Jared followed, ducked under branches but still got slapped in the face. He swatted them away with his free hand, held his pocket of berries with the other, and kept chasing after Kyle's bobbing pack and rifle. Jared's gait was awkward as his left hand clutched his food against his stomach. It was like swimming with only one arm.

They stopped on a rise. Jared gulped in air and glanced down, swearing quietly when he realized he'd lost some of his berries. He gripped the remaining stash and copied Kyle, who scanned the valley behind them. Trees. Trees. Tr—Jared snapped his attention back to a spot where a tree, a single tree, seemed to be swaying from more than just the wind. He pointed.

"I see it." A frown plowed furrows in Kyle's forehead. He took a drink of water and handed the canteen to Jared.

"A bear?" Jared drank and handed the container back.

"Let's hope so." He motioned for Jared to follow.

They dipped into the next valley at a brisk walk. The path opened into a clearing that was marshy on the south end and rose to a rocky ridge on the east. Kyle pointed at it. "I'd rather be up higher so we can see."

Jared's shirt was smeared with berry blood. He grabbed a dozen of the remaining berries and nibbled them while he followed. The way they almost bit him back with their flares of sourness as his teeth broke their skins bolstered him. Reminded him with each sharp burst that he was alive. In the city, he'd never given any thought to the sheer relief it was to still be breathing. He'd taken everything for granted. Food, safety, luxury. Life.

His heels were a bit sore, but seemed to be doing okay. He slowed as he examined his shoes, then hurried to catch up with Kyle. Plunged almost knee-deep in watery mud. Swore.

Kyle spun around, alarm on his face. When he saw Jared's predicament, he started to smile but wiped it away. "The trail goes around the mud hole, not through it."

"I got distracted." He strained to extract his foot from the sucking mud. It released him with a wet smacking sound and he almost fell onto his butt. He balanced on one leg and tried to shake off the worst of the mud, not caring that his jeans were slimed with muck, only that he hadn't lost his shoe. Or any of his berries. He gave Kyle a narrow look, expecting derision, but his face was blank. Then the frown returned.

Behind Jared, a sound, half snarl, half growl, sent shivers up and down his spine. He spun to see a wolverine at the spot where the path emerged from the trees. It was snarling and digging at the path, or maybe beside it. The animal paused and seemed to glare at them. It snarled, baring yellow fangs visible even from a distance. Then it moved down the path a yard and started digging again. Dirt flew up in a black curtain, almost obscuring the wolverine—if they were as rare as Kyle said it had to be that one they'd seen before.

This was the first time Jared had seen the wolverine clearly in the daytime. He hadn't realized it had stripes of dirty white running through its fur, like skunk stripes that had widened and had drooped onto the animal's sides instead of staying on its back. Its sheer power, the force with which it flung dirt, was mesmerizing.

Jared shook his head, hiked around the mud hole, flicking his foot every few steps to send droplets of mud spraying onto foliage. Behind him, the snarling continued. When he reached Kyle he said, "I don't think that animal likes me. It glares at me like it wants to tear into me. Kind of like you used to do. But it keeps hanging around. Also like you. Are you sure it's not your spirit guide or something?"

"It's not. I told you my last name was Badger, not Wolverine."

"Then it's *Wesakechak's* pet?"

Kyle's attention shifted from the wolverine to Jared. "You didn't see?"

"See what?"

"Guess you weren't looking outside any more."

"What?" Jared lifted one open palm in exasperation. "What did I miss?"

Kyle nodded toward the wolverine. "That isn't my spirit guide, but it's a kind of help that...that still messes with my mind. I'm trying to be thankful, to not wonder why." His gaze grew distant, as if he'd decided to pick this moment to figure out the puzzle.

Jared snapped his fingers in front of Kyle's face. "Dude. Just tell me."

Kyle blinked. "It's not my spirit guide, and it's not *Wesakechak's* pet." He sighed and pushed red-stained fingers through his hair, apparently frustrated by his inability to understand. "It's *Wesakechak*."

17

The Ridge

Kyle was on the move again, with long strides that made Jared half jog to keep up. He spoke to Kyle's back. "You expect me to believe that that wolverine is *Wesakechak?*" As insane as the idea sounded, it certainly explained the stink in the moss house.

"It *is Wesakechak*. As he was luring *Wîhtiko* away from the village, I saw it. He changed. One minute he was a tall warrior, the moonlight making his buckskins look silver, and the next he was a small black bundle with barely visible silver stripes. He raced away into the darkness. Led his enemy away from us."

Jared grabbed his arm and pulled Kyle to a stop. "If he's some kind of magical trickster, why doesn't he just kill *Wîhtiko?*"

Kyle yanked his arm free. "You saw the message he acted out last night. We broke it; we have to fix it. Not *Wesakechak*.

And the way he crossed his arms makes me think he's not going to help us much either, not anymore. Maybe someone isn't letting him." Kyle rubbed his neck and groaned. "I think we have to deal with all of it, including..." His lips silently formed the monster's name.

Jared felt revulsion congeal his features into a grimace. "But we can't do that. He doesn't expect us to do that, does he?"

"Yeah. I told you he's a *trickster*. *Wesakechak* makes deals and his stories are often funny. He, he isn't known for fighting things face to face. We should be thankful he's helped us as much as he has, and that he's trying to cover our trail right now."

"Why has he helped us at all?"

Kyle pulled free and marched along the trail.

Jared followed. "Why, Kyle?"

Kyle didn't slow down. If anything, his pace increased.

Jared broke into a jog. "It's because of me, isn't it?"

Kyle spun suddenly and Jared almost crashed into him, making him lose some more berries. Kyle glared. "Everything is about you, *Moniyaw*. You should know that by now."

"What the—What did I say? Don't shut me out here, Kyle. Don't start calling me *Moniyaw* again like I'm some kind of faceless...pale face." He blinked. Great. That made him sound like a jerk. Again.

"*Ffffuuu*" escaped Kyle's lips like air from a balloon. "Cover the well before I leave you here for the wolverine and *Wîhtiko* to fight over."

Well? Oh. The well of stupidity. Jared threw his hands

up in exasperation. Berries fell to the ground, except for a few he managed to save in his fist. He shouldered past Kyle and stalked along the trail. "Forget it. You don't want me to understand, that's fine. Maybe *Wesakechak* is as repulsed by me as you are. Maybe he can smell my city stink like *Wîhtiko* can. So much for being a tribe."

Jared felt the approaching vibrations more than he heard Kyle catch up. This time he was the one spun to a stop. Kyle's eyes were shadowed, black and stormy.

"You want to know the truth? You might not be my first choice for a tribesman, but I'm serious that we need to work together. I didn't answer you about *Wesakechak* because...I. Don't. Know. And I don't like not knowing. But me, I don't think he smells you like *Wîhtiko* does. The thought that he might be here to help *you*? Well, that bugs me. Okay? He's my people's legend, not yours." Kyle spun Jared back around and gave him a little push. "We don't have time for this."

Jared eyed the ground as he picked his way up the trail. "But maybe the only reason *Wesakechak* is helping us is because of you and your brave heart. Maybe he's helping because, like you said, you are one of his people, and *you're* here, trying to help me."

"Maybe."

The single word was grudging, as if Kyle wished he'd thought of that. A smile flitted across Jared's mouth and away. He plucked one berry from his fist and glanced back at the wolverine, visible only by the spray of dirt it was kicking up. If Kyle was right and that was *Wesakechak*, could he only change form into a wolverine? *Wesakechak*. It sounded almost like Whiskey Jack—the bird that had harassed them as they'd walked up the hill the first time. Had that been *Wesakechak* trying to warn them off?

Jared jogged to catch up. He mentioned his theory to Kyle, who shrugged. "Could be. All I know is, I wish I'd been able to understand everything he said."

"How much did you understand?"

Kyle squinted over his shoulder in the wolverine's direction. "A bit of the story, a few basic words like *eat, stay, morning*. I told you all this. It's the words in between, the ones I missed. They could've been important. And..." He sighed quietly.

"And what?"

"It's gonna sound stupid."

"It's your turn, don't you think? Why should I be the only stupid one?"

Kyle glanced over his shoulder, his expression half amused. "It's just that, I felt like he was disappointed in me. Not happy that I couldn't understand. And that he was offended by having to act out his message."

"You both need to get over it. I'm glad you understood any of what he said. My ancestors are Swedish. If we'd been whisked to a Viking spirit world, we'd be totally screwed. I don't know a single word in Swedish. Not one."

"Smorgasbord."

"What?"

"A Swedish word. Smorgasbord. It's a buffet or something."

"Okay. I've heard of that. But, see? You know more Swedish than I do."

Kyle snorted. "You have to ask yourself: Is it a good thing that the only Swedish word I know has to do with things getting eaten?"

Jared couldn't think of a reply. His stomach grumbled, thankfully too quietly for Kyle to hear. Jared patted the front of his shirt but no red currants clung to any creases; all he had left were the few squished in his left fist. He licked his palms and fingers, savoring the last remnants as they reached the top of the ridge.

The valley dipped off to their right, the marsh directly below them now. The patches of water separated by islands of stunted gray trees, grass, and mud, looked like a maze. A pair of ducks paddled across the largest pond. The blue was a rippling mirror that made the reflections of the trees quiver.

Off to the left wind rustled through a dense forest of spruce trees with barren lower branches and sparse upper ones. The sunlight fell in stripes across the heavy underbrush. Leafy plants poked up from moss and deadfall. Here and there exposed roots looked ready to trip the clumsy.

The trail along the ridge was clear. So was the sky, except for the haze in the west and the single plume of smoke being dispersed by the wind. The ashy smell clogged Jared's throat.

He glanced at Kyle, who scanned the valley. The wind piped between them.

And whispered Jared's name.

They spun toward each other, spoke simultaneously. "Did you hear that?" They both paused, then both spoke again. "I heard my name."

They stared at each other for a minute, eyes wide, reflecting faces full of uncertainty. "I heard my name on the wind. This is the third time," Jared whispered.

"And I heard mine, but it's the first time," Kyle replied. A scowl dropped over his features. "A story. I remember Moshum telling me...to never go looking if the wind calls my name."

Jared wiped at his mouth. "Why?"

"Because...it's *Wîhtiko* hoping to lure you away."

Frantic thrashing startled Jared. He spun to see the pair of ducks flapping into the sky and over them, necks stretched as if they were racing each other. He scanned the marsh.

"He's gone," Kyle said. Before Jared could ask who, Kyle spoke again. "*Wesakechak.*"

He grabbed Jared's arm. "Our names. Now the ducks being scared off. We need to get out of sight." He dragged Jared behind a tree and crouched. He swung his rifle from shoulder to hands and squinted along the ridge.

"Shouldn't we be moving?" Jared asked, back pressed against the scaly tree trunk.

Kyle nodded. "Follow me."

He kept low, darted from tree to shrub to fallen tree to the next upright one. Jared imitated him. He felt like he'd just run a mile, even though it had barely been ten yards. He paused to ask a question but Kyle was already moving again.

They hopscotched through the forest, the ridge always in sight. Jared worked to stay as quiet as possible, to not snap brittle twigs or step on fallen branches. They made good progress, though Jared wished they could move faster. The only sound was the wind as it moaned and whistled through the treetops. Was that his name again? Jared shivered and sped up.

The next time he caught up, Kyle pulled him down and pointed. The ridge had curved a bit, allowing them to look back along its spine. Someone was climbing up the hill, pausing, climbing, turning his head one way, then toward them, face lifted to the sky.

Smelling.

Jared's heartbeat thundered wildly. He turned to Kyle, who was wide-eyed. Kyle whispered, "Time to run. Away from the ridge. Maybe we'll lose it in the forest."

Kyle nudged him. "Go."

Jared pushed off, stumbled, then burst into a sprint. Dodged around trees. Leapt logs. Brushed past shrubs, tall weeds. A root tripped him. He sprawled onto a bed of moss.

Rifle still in one hand, Kyle pulled him up. Gave him a small shove. "Faster."

Sunlight flashed through the trees. Into Jared's eyes. He careened off a gangly spruce and stumbled sideways, ribs aching. Lungs heaving. He kept moving, slower, though he tried to urge his legs to go faster.

Kyle yanked him to a halt. Ahead, the forest seemed to be thinning to either side, but they couldn't see beyond. More marsh? Both trembling, they searched the forest behind them.

They saw it at the same time. A flash of pale brown in the filtered light.

Kyle moaned. "It's catching up."

"How? It crept up the hill so slowly."

"When it was smelling. Maybe it sped up when it noticed our movement."

Adrenaline surged. Jared bolted toward the clearing. Kyle kept pace. Side by side, they raced. Veering around trees. Leaping simultaneously over logs. Kyle eased ahead three steps. His rifle broke branches as he cleared another log. Jared jumped.

And was clotheslined by Kyle's outstretched arm. He would have fallen had Kyle not grabbed his deerskin shirt and held firm.

"What the—?" Jared's eyes bulged. He clamped his mouth shut.

They hadn't been running toward a marsh. They stood on a neck of land that jutted out over a lake. Eight or ten yards below, wind-tossed waves beat against a base they couldn't see without leaning over the cliff's edge. This was the highest point of land around the lake. From here, the land sloped down either direction. On the far side the trees grew right up to the shore. The dark, moon-shaped lake was small but looked deep.

Behind them, crashing footsteps and breaking branches grew louder.

"We're done," Kyle said. His shoulders sagged.

"No. You are *not* going to die because of me. Not today, anyway." Jared grabbed the rifle from a slackened grip. He tucked it behind the nearest tree. "Take off your backpack.

We're going swimming."

"I'm not a very good swimmer."

"I am." Jared grasped their only thread of hope. "And with any luck, that thing doesn't swim at all."

Kyle shrugged his backpack off. Jared stowed it beside the rifle.

"I'm...not sure about this." Kyle peered into the forest at their back.

"Got a better idea? Will the rifle kill it?"

"No."

"That's what I figured, or you would've suggested it a long time ago." Jared seized Kyle's wrist and pulled him, unresisting, twenty steps back. "Okay. Run, and when you jump get as much air under you as possible. Like long jump on track day. The farther out, the less likely something nasty is close to the surface. Land feet first."

"This is not safe."

Jared snagged Kyle's collar and pulled him down a few inches. "Probably not, but it's safer than waiting around to visit with that monster."

Kyle nodded. His shoulders sagged. Jared felt a tug of despair. If Kyle gave up, they were sunk. He poked the broad chest and sneered. "Haven't you ever wanted to jump off a cliff and scream 'Geronimo'?"

As he'd hoped, Kyle's head snapped up to reveal a pissed expression.

"That's better." Jared grinned. "On three."

The crashing was so close, Jared didn't dare look. Rapidly he counted, "Three. Two. One!"

They charged toward the cliff. Faster. Faster.

Jared planted his foot at the edge of the precipice and launched. Arms and legs windmilled. When he felt the fall begin, he closed his legs, pointed his toes, and glued his arms to his sides. The water hurtled toward him.

The last thing he heard was Kyle shouting, "*Wesakechak!*"

18

Water

As soon as he hit the water, Jared went starfish, spreading his arms and legs to slow descent. Then he started kicking. Above him, the murky light swished with the waves. It grew bluish as he ascended. A single red berry floated and bobbed. Glowed like a ruby.

Jared swept his arms sideways and turned, looking for Kyle. The wind was churning up the water too much to see any distance. He broke surface and inhaled loudly. Small waves slapped his face. He spotted Kyle's camo jacket, just below the surface.

Using a sidestroke, Jared swam the few yards, fighting dread with each stroke. Kyle was face down, so he rolled him over. *Be okay, Kyle. You have to be okay.* Water dribbled from his slack mouth. He was unconscious. Jared swore. *Focus, moron. You know what to do.* He started treading water and extended Kyle's neck. Deep-water resuscitation. He'd taken the course before a trip to Cuba. *Thanks, Mom. Now let it work.* Thankfully, he needed to puff only two breaths into Kyle's mouth to get him breathing. He coughed, sputtered out some water, but didn't wake.

Jared scanned to find the nearest shore. His gaze rose like an elevator to the top of the cliff. *Wîhtiko* stood at the edge, flailed at some broken branches, then raised arms to the sky.

No. *Nononono.* If it screamed, Jared knew he was dead. He'd freeze. Sink. Drown.

Wîhtiko tilted its head back.

Jared took a deep breath and ducked under. He grabbed the back of Kyle's collar and towed him through the water. A diffused far-away sound sent shivers through the water to tickle Jared's skin. Cold rippled around him but he was able to keep moving.

When he ran out of air, he released Kyle, clamped hands over his ears, and surfaced. He gulped oxygen and skimmed his gaze along the promontory. *Wîhtiko* was moving, heading clockwise around the lake. Jared changed directions and began swimming toward the shore, south of the cliff, if the sun's position was any indication. He continued to tow Kyle, but reverted to a sidestroke for more speed.

They were almost to shore when Kyle started to struggle. Jared snapped, "Hold still. Relax or I won't be able to help."

"W-what happened?"

Jared's foot bumped bottom. He stood, gripped Kyle under his arms, and backed onto shore, dragging Kyle. "You must have hit the water at an angle. It knocked you out."

With every step, Kyle's bulk became harder to maneuver. Their feet were still in water when Jared collapsed beside Kyle, puffing. "Seems *Wîhtiko* isn't fond of water. But it turns out that being under water stops its screams from working."

"It screamed. So I was frozen?"

"Probably. It didn't matter with you floating. I was able to pull you anyway." Jared squinted into Kyle's eyes but didn't see anything weird about his pupils; maybe he didn't have a concussion. He hoped not. A dazed and confused Kyle would be their death warrant.

"You saved me." Kyle's voice was a rasp.

Jared lay back and rested one sopping arm across his forehead. "Don't get too excited about that. We've got to find the strength to move. It's headed around the lake. Fortunately, it has to go most of the way around. Unfortunately, it isn't a big lake."

Kyle craned his neck. "We're near the base of the cliff."

"Yes, but it's easy to scale here. It's not even two meters up the bank."

"I can hardly feel my legs. Go get my pack. The rifle."

Jared sat up, bent his knees to get out of the cold water. "Are you crazy? We've got to run."

"Without the rifle all I have is a skinning knife. Even the canteen is with the pack."

Jared felt a pocket and pulled out his iPod and earbuds. "The compass is gone. *Great.* I sure don't have anything useful." His fist tightened around them. He should throw them away but...that felt like admitting they'd never get back. Keeping them felt like a promise to himself, that he'd get

KAREN BASS

to listen to his tunes again. He stuffed the buds and device back in their pocket. "Fine. I'll go. Find your legs before I get back."

He pushed to his feet and jumped. Grabbed a root and pulled himself up, feet scrambling for purchase and almost getting tangled in more roots. He dragged himself over the lip of the bank and rolled away on a cushion of moss. It seemed to cradle him, offer him a bed. Rest. He needed to rest.

"You okay?" Kyle called up.

"Yeah." Jared lurched to his feet and started up the incline. The higher he climbed the more their desperation snapped at his heels. Minutes later he was at the top of the cliff. Wheezing, he shouldered the pack and held the rifle stock just ahead of the trigger. No way he wanted to accidentally fire it, if that were even possible.

Then he ran. Down an animal trail that descended parallel to the cliff. Each step jolted up his shins. He watched the trail, afraid if he looked away he'd fall. Over a root. Under a branch.

He crashed into Kyle, who had climbed the bank overlooking the water. The rifle was wedged between them, muzzle pointed to the sky. "Got my legs. You want me to carry the rifle?"

"Yes." He stepped back and handed it over gladly. "Which way?"

"Still southeast."

Kyle took a drink from the canteen and handed it to Jared. "Last of the water. Hope we find a stream."

Jared drained the canteen. The last few drops landed on

his deerskin shirt. "What about the lake?"

"No. I saw *Wîhtiko* moving along the far shore. I don't want to risk it seeing us."

Jared shouldered the pack. "I'll carry this until you're sure you're feeling better."

Kyle nodded and attached the canteen to its O-ring on the pack. "Listen. About back there in the water ..." He straightened, gaze dark and solemn. "*Kinanâskomitin, nisimis.*"

"And that means ...?"

"I thank you, little brother."

Jared was still wet, and shivering now that he wasn't moving. But warmth bubbled up and a smile stole over his lips. "Stop reminding me that I'm small."

"The better word is puny." Kyle hiked away.

"Huh. You're welcome." Jared was still smiling as he tramped behind. Which was crazy, considering what was following them.

Soon enough, the smile was nothing more than a memory. Whenever the terrain allowed, Kyle broke into a jog. The brutal pace he set left no room for smiling. Grimacing was all Jared could manage. Though his clothes remained damp and uncomfortable, sweat dripped off his brow. He held onto the shoulder strap of the pack and slogged behind, forcing himself to keep pace. To jog when his legs wobbled like he was on a trampoline.

On and on through endless forest. The only thing that changed was the slant of the sun's rays. A sundial for those who could read it. What he wouldn't give for a simple street sign: *Wîhtiko's* Lair This Way. Or Hill of Doom, Right Lane.

They stumbled to a halt by a trickle of water. Jared stared, certain this was good but unable to remember why.

Kyle croaked, "Canteen." He held out his hand.

Jared shook himself and turned so Kyle could unclip the canteen. Still following Kyle, he skidded down the small embankment and dropped to his knees by the water. He doubled over and scooped cold water into his mouth, not caring that it tasted of silt. He drank handfuls of the stuff until suddenly his stomach convulsed and the water spewed back into the stream. On all fours he dry heaved over the water for a moment, then fell back on his heels.

Kyle handed him the canteen. "Try again. Smaller sips. Don't barf into it."

Jared wiped his mouth and did as Kyle said. When his stomach gurgled he handed the canteen back. "I can't do it, Kyle. Can't move. I'm done."

"No chance. We keep going."

"To where? I lost the compass in the lake. Do you even know where you are?"

"Remember how we talked about feeling the hill? That shadow inside is growing again, getting darker and bigger as we get closer."

A shudder ran through Jared's frame. "I'll take your word for it." But now that Kyle had mentioned it, he realized he could feel that lurking presence too. Their own true north in this place of spirits, tricksters, and monsters. It struck Jared that *Wîhtiko* seemed like some kind of zombie. *We're caught in a twisted episode of* The Walking Dead, *but we don't have a weapon that can kill the zombie. At least in video games and movies you can defend yourself.* "Do you think it's still following us?"

"Yeah."

That drove Jared to his feet. One knee gave out and he braced himself against Kyle's solid frame. Found his feet. Straightened with a groan.

"Us, we have to trust that *Wesakechak* is still out there, too. Still trying to cover our scent. I think that's why he keeps changing into a wolverine. You know how bad it smells."

"The better to cover my city stink."

"Exactly."

Jared took a tentative step and surprised himself by staying upright. He didn't resist when Kyle tugged at the backpack, slid it off his shoulders and settled it on his own. With a nod of encouragement, Kyle splashed across the stream. Jared followed, slipped on a rock but regained his footing.

"For the record," he said to Kyle's back, "I've never been a big fan of nature and this trip hasn't changed my mind."

"When we get home, you can spend a few days with me at our moose camp and see that it's fun."

"Nature isn't fun. It's a freaking Godzilla looking to crush you the way we crush ants."

"And the city is a freaking jungle where the weak get a slab of concrete for a bed and have to dumpster dive for food."

Snarking with Kyle restored some of Jared's energy. They continued on, marching and sniping, until Jared couldn't think of a comeback. He lagged behind, sped up when he realized it. After that, it took all his concentration to keep up with Kyle, whose energy seemed boundless. And *he* was the one knocked unconscious by the water. Maybe it had been the swim to shore, and lugging a zonked-out elephant, that had drained Jared's energy.

His stomach gnawed at itself. He barely noticed when they stepped into a clearing. Kyle gripped his shoulder and he blinked. Looked around. The hill loomed directly ahead of them. But between them and it sprawled a marsh, the biggest one they'd come across.

"Around will take a long time," Kyle remarked.

"You want to go through it? Is it safe? It might be like the Dead Marshes in *The Lord of the Rings*, full of spirits waiting to lure us to our deaths."

"Sounds fun. Let's go."

That jolted Jared to alertness. "Are you nuts?"

"Across will be faster." Kyle produced a macabre grin. "Lured into drowning has to be better than being ripped to pieces."

Jared shivered. "You're crazy."

"Said the madman to the lunatic. Where's the guy who pissed me off and got me to jump off a cliff? Let him come out and play."

Jared clamped his hands over his ears. "Just go."

The gruesome smile returned. Kyle hopped across to the first spit of land, only a yard from the shore. Jared followed, landing on soft ground that squished with every step. Mosquitoes returned to dip and dive and bite. The strip of land narrowed, became spongier, then widened into a more solid mass again.

Halfway across that islet, they passed through a cloud of vibrating dots. Several got into Jared's mouth and up his nose. He spat and snorted. "What are those stupid little bugs? Blackflies?"

"Nah. Blackflies are bigger and they bite like rattlesnakes. Those bugs are no-see-ums. They've never bothered me when they're swarming like that."

Jared picked his way over a few puddles. He scratched at a small red spot near his wrist but couldn't say when he'd gotten it. Probably from one of those no-see-ums. He got it. No-see-um. Very clever.

They paused at the edge of this islet and considered the runnel of water between them and the next patch of land. It was a narrow, shallow channel; they shared a glance, shrugged simultaneously, and splashed across. The mud weakly sucked at Jared's shoes.

Kyle pointed across the water to a moose that lifted its head from under the water to watch them. Jared wanted to ask if they traveled in herds but didn't want to sound stupid. The moose plunged its head into the water again.

As their path meandered through the bog, Jared began to think "around" would have been just as fast. He'd been so intent on watching for a dry path that he hadn't checked their surroundings, but when he peered both ways he saw they were in the middle of a long valley floor that looked to be all marsh. Kyle was right again. Freaking annoying habit.

At least they were closing in on the eastern shore. Another channel. Another splash through stagnant water. This time the water was waist deep. Jared waddled through the sludge, struggled up onto the next island. And sank into a mud hole.

He felt cold slime sucking him down. He tried to pull free. The mud oozed up over his knees. Alarm shivered along his spine. Jared strained to free one leg. "Kyle!"

"Come on." Kyle turned. "What are you—?"

Jared sank another five inches. Fear took hold. He strained forward, stretched out his hand. "Help! I'm sinking."

19

Mud

As cold as the freezing scream of *Wîhtiko*, the liquid cement held Jared's legs in its depths. He struggled. And sank.

"Stop moving," Kyle said. "That only makes it worse."

Jared forced himself to stillness. But when he was still, he could feel the slow descent. Feel himself being sucked deeper. The mud and water were almost up to his crotch. Panic gripped his muscles. His heart bounced off his ribs like a trapped fly. He gave a mighty jerk. And sank more. The mud smelled like he'd taken a dump. "Tell me what to do, Kyle." The words quavered.

"I told you. Don't move."

Kyle set aside his pack and rifle, and moved behind a gray skeletal tree. He eyed its height, squinted at Jared, then lunged against the trunk, like a hulking football defender attacking the opposing team's line. Jared focused completely on Kyle, the only way he knew to keep his dread under wraps. The roots lifted. When the tree was leaning at close to a forty-five-degree angle, Kyle circled around, got under the scrawny trunk, and pulled. Through clenched teeth he said, "When it gets in reach, grab hold."

Kyle's face screwed up with effort. His grunts and keening made him sound like an Olympic weightlifter. Jared watched the trunk slowly bend lower. He figured he had exactly one shot, because as soon as he moved he would sink more. When it finally came within reach, Jared shot his arms into the air and latched onto the dead tree.

"Got it!"

"Don't let go." Kyle repositioned himself with a shoulder under the trunk and began to push up.

Jared clung to the knobbed wood. The tree bent like an archer's bow, and he had the ridiculous vision of being launched into the air like a cartoon figure. He might have laughed if it weren't for the slight movement that grabbed his attention. "I think it's working."

Kyle only grunted in reply, kept pushing, more sideways than up. Jared's body started to rise from the muck. He tightened his grip but could still feel sweat slicking his palms. "Hurry," he whispered under his breath.

The tree seemed to groan. It swung to the right a little. Jared slipped. Gritting his teeth, he shifted his hands, twisted. Looked down at the churned mud, gray-brown with swirls of black. He glanced over his shoulder, wondering how many other mud holes they'd missed by sheer chance.

"Crap," he blurted.

On the western shore of the bog, a man stepped from shadow to sunlight. From this distance it was hard to tell who it was. Light buckskins. Dark hair. Jared's stomach and fists clenched. A knot dug into his palm but he held tight.

He looked away from the figure. "Hurry. We have company."

Kyle's head jerked around but he didn't stop pushing. His face folded into a prolonged squint. His shoulders bunched and he shoved with all his might. "Aahhhhhh!"

The trunk snapped. The loud crack sounded like a rifle shot. Jared thudded sideways onto soft ground, broken limb clutched in his cramped fingers. Kyle grabbed his wrists and hauled him free of the mud hole, then fell to the ground beside him. For several moments they both heaved and panted.

"Can you tell who it is?" Jared gasped between words.

Kyle propped himself up on his elbows. "No, but I think *Wîhtiko* would be moving toward us."

Jared's stomach relaxed a little. "So it's *Wesakechak?*"

"Probably wondering why we're moving so slow. Whenever he shows up, his enemy isn't far behind."

Jared rolled onto his side to face Kyle. "Why didn't you just grab my hands and pull to begin with? Why use the dead tree?"

"Hard to tell where the edge of a hole like that starts. I couldn't get too close." Kyle kept his attention glued to the far side of the bog. "You scared me. I've never seen someone sink that fast."

"Scared *you?* I almost crapped, not that you'd notice. Dude, that mud smells like diarrhea." Jared sat up. "I swear this place hates me."

"Could be." Kyle pushed up, raised his knees and rested his arms on them. He was still breathing like he'd swum a relay race. He eyed Jared's mud-slathered legs. "Still planning on never washing those fancy jeans?"

Jared wrinkled his nose as he ran a finger along his slimed shins. He flicked the mud at Kyle. It splatted onto his cheek. He wiped it off and started laughing. Jared joined in. For several minutes they hooted and laughed so hard Jared's side ached.

When the laughter faded away, Jared asked, "What were we laughing about?"

"No idea."

The hill was visible through a gap in the trees. From here the trees populating its slope were black and ominous. Jared could swear the thing was glowering at them. Daring them to return. His throat tightened and he worked to swallow as the hill seemed to cast an invisible shadow over the valley.

Kyle stood, offered his hand and pulled Jared up.

"What are you, freaking Captain America?" Jared snorted. "Don't you ever get tired?" He glanced at the hill again, afraid to ask if Kyle was feeling the same foreboding.

Kyle rubbed his neck. "I'm tired. But we can rest when we get home."

"I will sleep for a week."

"Just what I'd expect a city boy to say." The smile tugging at one corner of Kyle's mouth said he was trying to get a rise from Jared. Get him stirred up and moving. Or maybe it was a dig to repay him for that Geronimo remark.

"Jerk," Jared replied mildly. He took a few steps and the movement caused muddy stink to waft upwards. *It gets worse and worse.* He nodded toward the hill. "Will we get there today?"

"It'll be a long day but I'm hoping to get to our moose camp." Kyle kept glancing to the west. It was making Jared nervous.

"Why the camp?" he asked.

"Do you really want to spend another night on the hill? *That hill?*"

"Good point." Maybe Kyle was feeling the same dread.

"The spring will give us fresh water and it's well hidden. Should be a safe place to sleep."

"*Should be* is all we're going to get, I suppose." Jared's stomach coiled into knots again. A quick glance confirmed that *Wesakechak* was still on the western shore. Jared realized that Kyle was waiting for him to be able to move. Tired or not, the tension seemed to jiggle through Kyle's long legs. He really was as tireless as Captain America. Kyle peered past Jared, lips pressed tight. Jared's stomach squeezed so tight he wondered which end would explode first.

Willing energy into his legs, he jogged to the edge of the island and leapt over the yard-wide channel to the next one. Movement injected some adrenaline into his system. He jogged faster. This islet was joined to another by a spit of soggy land. Jared leapt over the worst of it. One more leap across one final runnel brought him to the shore.

Kyle was only a step behind. "I thought you'd want to wade through water to get rid of the worst of the mud."

"No way. Smell it, Kyle. If this mud doesn't rid me of my city stink, nothing will."

KAREN BASS

Kyle slapped him on the back. "Hope so. And look at that embankment. Our luck is changing. Pineapple weed is edible."

He plucked some low weeds from the gravel slope and gave the plants to Jared. "Flowers and stems are best."

"These tiny yellowish things that are shaped like pineapples are flowers? Wonder where they got the name?"

Kyle grabbed himself a fistful of the weeds. "Wonder while we walk."

"That was sarcasm." Getting only a grunt in reply, Jared twirled a single feathery leaf stalk, then took a bite. Weird. It even tasted a bit like pineapple, which he'd never particularly liked. It was amazing what a stomach would suffer when it was hungry enough. He took another bite and grimaced as they joined the forest shadows.

20

Trails

Jared couldn't tell how long he'd been racing through the forest, desperate to keep Kyle in sight. Desperate to put distance between them and *Wîhtiko*.

The adrenaline rush from the bog wore thin. Jared's stomach rumbled as he ducked under yet another spruce branch. Tiny pineapple weeds couldn't fill the growing void. Quite possibly a whole pig roasted Hawaiian luau style wouldn't be enough. He could almost smell the succulent pork and the fresh pineapple.

He closed his eyes and stumbled to a stop, wondering if he had actually smelled something cooking. He could pick out the forest fire's scent—roasted tree—but nothing else. Even the mud was stinking less now that it was drying, flaking off. His energy escaped with a sigh. He staggered to the side, under sweeping branches and onto spongy ground. Moss. He fell onto it, wheezing quietly.

No way *Wîhtiko* could smell him anymore. He stank of mud and sweat. No trace of anything city. Maybe he could rest for a few moments and—

Something kicked his shin. Kept kicking it.

"Get lost." He rolled over.

Something kicked his butt. Hard.

"Ouch! What the—" Jared jolted upright. He squinted as his bleary vision cleared to reveal Kyle glaring at him with black-hole eyes.

Kyle kicked him again. He scuttled out of boot range, but Kyle just swatted a branch aside and followed. "What the hell are you doing? I had to backtrack when I realized you weren't behind me. I might not have found you if I hadn't heard you snoring. Flat on your back, snoring loud as a chainsaw."

"Snoring? I barely remember stopping." Jared flopped onto his back, arms spread wide. "I can't keep running like this, Kyle. Can't. I'm starving, but my stomach's so balled up in knots that I'd probably barf up anything I ate. I'm done."

"You've said that before and found the strength to keep going." Kyle bent over and hauled Jared to his feet. "Find the strength now."

"It's gone. It's flown to Hawaii and is enjoying a luau."

Jared's knees started to buckle but Kyle kept him upright, pulled Jared's arm up and around his neck and held tight. Clamped his other arm around his waist and half dragged, half carried Jared back to the trail. The rifle stock pressed against Jared's elbow.

"God, I'm so hungry." He groaned quietly and tried to imitate Kyle's walking motion. Their thighs bumped with each step. "Can't you shoot something so we can eat?"

"I've told you—"

"Rifles are too noisy. I remember."

Branches swatted Jared's arm as they made their way along the path. One scratched his cheek. He flinched away, turned his face against Kyle's chest. This was so freaking humiliating, being hauled along like a child. "Stop." His voiced was muffled against the camouflage jacket. He repeated it louder. Kyle stopped.

Jared wormed his way free from Kyle's hold. "I'll walk."

"You said you were done."

"Well, I'm not about to let you drag me along like some kind of northern Alberta Tarzan."

Kyle snorted. "Me, I'm not enjoying this, either, you know. And I sure as hell don't think of you as Jane."

Jared stared blankly, then realized what he was saying. Tarzan had carried away Jane because he thought she was hot. "I never—"

"You're kind of like the monkey, though."

"The monkey? You mean the chimp he called Leopard or Cheetah or something? How do you figure that?" He half smiled, expecting Kyle's weird humor to make him laugh.

"You're more likely to panic than do anything useful." Kyle flapped his arms. "Eeee! Eeee! Eeee!" He poked Jared's chest. "And you always find new ways to get into trouble."

Jared pressed his lips together as irritation bubbled up, any thought of laughter gone. He wanted to say a hundred nasty things in reply, but couldn't force even one past his teeth. Kyle was right. Though he was an asshole to say it.

Jared turned and stalked down the trail, fists clenched as tightly as his jaw. He swung his arms and powered along the path with Kyle trailing. He refused to look back.

He stumbled once, felt a hand on his arm and shook it off. He wanted to run, but knew that would be asking to trip and land face-first in a patch of nettle or something equally nasty. Maybe this place hated him because Kyle hated him. Maybe, since it was a spirit world of some kind, it could sense Kyle's vibes and turn them into the land itself wanting to hurt him—the way a guitar's sound hole picks up the notes from the plucked strings and amplifies them.

"Hey," Kyle said.

Jared kept marching. Kyle grabbed the back of his deer-skin shirt and yanked him to a standstill. A big hand clamped onto his arm. He turned and glared.

Kyle said, "This trail is swinging back north. We have to go this way." He jerked his head to the right. His forehead wrinkled and his brows drew together. "Look, Jared, I didn't mean what I said."

"Yes, you did. And why not? It's true."

"It might've been true yesterday, but not today."

"I did find trouble. The mud hole. Napping when a monster is chasing us. I told you to leave me."

"Shut up. Either one of us could've fallen into that mud. The nap, well, we both need rest. I forget it's hard for you to keep up to these long legs. You've mostly been keeping up pretty good, so much that I keep forgetting you were in that plane crash—getting back to normal after an accident takes time and I shouldn't expect you to keep up. But you are. I wasn't pissed at you. I was worried." Kyle started to run his fingers over his head and stopped, palm capping his mussed hair. "Kokum gets mad at me when she's worried. Do your parents do that?"

"Sort of. What's your point?"

"You got me to jump off a cliff by pissing me off. Me, I thought I could get you moving the same way. I didn't think you'd believe what I was saying." Before Jared could process that, Kyle took a step onto another trail, one Jared hadn't even noticed. Kyle beckoned with a wave. "Come on. We're almost there."

Kyle walked a half-dozen steps down the trail and looked back. "I'm sorry. Okay? Let's make tracks."

"You're an asshole."

"That's the pot calling the kettle black."

Jared started down the path. "What does that mean?"

Kyle resumed walking. "Over a campfire, pots and kettle both get pitch black. Kokum says it means that, um, it takes one to know one." He cast a grin over his shoulder.

"No one except you has ever called me that," Jared said.

"To your face maybe."

Jared curled his lip at Kyle's back but didn't bother to argue. Everything he'd worried about—how he didn't want to step in water that might ruin his shoes, getting a grass stain on his raw jeans—was all so pointless. What did anything matter when survival was the issue?

As if on cue, Jared's stomach rumbled.

It didn't take long for the energy burst to drain away. The afternoon became a blur—moving, always moving. He drank water when Kyle handed him the canteen, ate when Kyle pointed out another edible plant. Mostly wild roses, or rather, the little bulbs that Kyle called rose hips. Wherever the forest thinned enough for sunlight to caress the underbrush, roses grew. They'd stop long enough to pluck any rose hips they could see and then eat as they walked. Everything that went into his mouth tasted as crappy as that mud had smelled.

Kyle had lied. They weren't close. They walked for hours. Or maybe days or weeks. Jared couldn't tell. Couldn't think. Had they really been at *Wesakechak's* moss house only this morning? Had they really jumped off a cliff to get away from *Wîhtiko*? Was it closing in again? Slinking through the forest like a shadow. And all the while, the specter of the hill swelled to tower over them. Trapped between the hill and a monster.

What was *Wîhtiko* really? It couldn't be a zombie. They were always so easy to kill in the movies. A single shot to the head and you're done.

Jared walked into Kyle's backpack. Bounced onto his butt. He swiveled his head, took in the surroundings. A clearing. Alertness splashed over him like cold water. He sprang to his feet. The clearing. Kyle's moose camp clearing.

Kyle's shoulders were heaving as if he couldn't get enough oxygen. Drowning in twilight. Jared stepped up beside him. A rose bush prickled against his shin.

Kyle whispered, "I didn't think I'd ever see her again."

His kokum's fire was ten steps away. She was sleeping on her side near the flames, one arm tucked under her head as a pillow. As if she sensed their presence, she opened her eyes, shifted so she was kneeling. Her gaze roamed the area. Fixed on them. Widened.

"She can see us?" Jared asked.

"Looks like."

"She looks different."

Kyle scowled as he examined her but said nothing.

Jared stepped high over the rose bush, approached the fire, stopped a yard away. "She doesn't look so gray. So... ghosty. And the fire. It has some color now, too."

All the colors were identifiable but muted. She was wearing a green and brown camouflage jacket, a near match to Kyle's. Jeans tucked into hiking boots now had an indigo hue. The laces on her boots were red.

"What's it mean, dude?" Jared turned to Kyle. His face was the color of ashes.

Kyle shook his head. "Me, I...I think all her praying, or the sweetgrass...something is opening a door between our world and this one."

"Awesome." Jared gave a mini fist-pump of victory. "So we just need to wait a bit longer and we can walk back into our own lives."

Kyle turned a horrified face toward Jared. "Are you crazy? If we can walk through this, this *doorway*, then so can *Wîhtiko*."

21

Decisions

Kyle dropped to his knees before the faded vision of his grandmother. She looked like a colorized silent movie, the hues not vibrant enough to be real. But she didn't have that celluloid flicker as she stood and reached to the sky in a gesture of prayer. The breeze seemed to whisper, *Mercy.*

Have mercy. Save them.

Jared crouched beside Kyle. "Did you hear that? I thought I heard her. Something."

Kyle didn't respond. His features were glazed, like a porcelain doll's, glistening brown cheeks, unseeing eyes. *Don't freak on me now, dude.* Jared shook Kyle's shoulder. No response. Shook harder.

Slowly, the porcelain doll came to life. Kyle turned his head. His voice was cracked and bleeding. "They're...my family. My only. Family."

"What do you mean? You said you have cousins. You must have a mom." Jared bit the inside of his lip. Kyle had never mentioned his mom. Not once.

"Don't live...with cousins. Mom. Gone." Kyle raised a trembling arm. "My family. We've led *Wîhtiko* straight back to them, Jared."

The pain in the words pounded him. Jared sank onto the ground and hugged his knees to his chest. For several long minutes he watched Kyle's kokum pray. She looked exhausted. Like she was living on nothing more than prayer. She looked like Jared felt. Had they been living on prayers, too? Were her prayers the reason *Wesakechak* had helped them?

He was so freaking tired he could barely think. Couldn't find his way through the haze fogging his brain. The grayed-out woman standing before them was praying, yet still she managed to seem proud. Tall. She looked intense, like she wouldn't end her vigil until her grandson was returned to her. Like standing when she was exhausted could somehow give him strength. Did Jared's grandmother even know he was missing? Was she sitting in some little maritime chapel praying for *his* return?

Save them, the wind had whispered. Not just Kyle. *Save them.*

A flood blurred Jared's vision, but didn't spill its banks. He squeezed his eyes shut. Wiped them with the back of his hand, then rubbed his hand on the shoulder of his deerskin shirt, splotched by that far-off mud hole. The dried slime barely stank anymore.

Jared swung around so he blocked Kyle's view of his kokum. A frown slowly pulled Kyle's eyebrows together as his focus shifted to Jared. "What?"

"Did you mean what you said this morning at the village?"

"What did I say?"

"You said we're a tribe, you and me. At least while we're here."

Kyle gave a shrug and nod at the same time.

"Good. I'm kind of new at this tribe thing. You know, thinking of other people." That didn't bring even the tiniest smile to Kyle's tight-pressed mouth. Jared licked his lips. "But it means watching each other's backs, right? Standing together?"

Another nod. Kyle's brown eyes were murky, uncertain. He tilted his head to peer over Jared's shoulder at his kokum. With longing and fear and hunger.

"Here's the thing." Jared inhaled deeply, trying to suck in the courage and strength of the almost-there woman at his back. "You wouldn't leave me. You made me run when I wanted to stop. You kept me going. I'd have been a *Wîhtiko* snack long ago if you hadn't stuck by me."

"What's your point?"

Jared half smiled at the memory of saying that to Kyle not too long ago. Or maybe years ago. It was all blurring together. Nights. Days. Endless walking. Running. Living off freaking rose hips.

"My point is that running isn't working. *Wîhtiko* just keeps on coming." Kyle sat up a bit straighter. Jared had his attention now. "My point is that *this* is your tribe." He pointed with his thumb over his shoulder. "And I'm your tribe, too. So I want to help you protect them."

A look brimming with doubt settled on Kyle's features. "What are you going to do?"

"Not just me. Us. *We* are going to get some rest so our brains will actually work, then we're going to figure out a way to beat *Wîhtiko*."

22

Uphill

"Beat *Wîhtiko*?" Kyle's eyebrows arched toward his hairline.

"*Yes!*" Jared poured every drop of conviction he had into that one word. "*Wîhtiko* is going down, dude. We are not going to let that thing hurt your family."

A smile claimed Kyle's lips.

Jared scowled. "What?"

"You, you're a decent guy when you think about other people."

"That right? Well, annoyingly, you're a decent guy all the time." Jared stood in slow motion. "But don't let it go to your head. It's already bigger than the rest of you." He swayed. Then he held out his hand, staggered one step back as he pulled Kyle to his feet.

"You're falling-down tired." Kyle gave him a poke that

made him sway again.

"Eyes like an eagle." Jared rubbed his face. "We'll rest. You must be more tired than you look."

Kyle gave a nod and scanned the clearing. He was always doing that whenever they stopped. Like his eyes were ADD or something, but in this case Jared was glad of it. Glad of the fleeting sense that someone was watching out for him. Glad he had Kyle in his tribe, out here in the weird, weird wilderness.

"Let's retreat to the spring." Kyle gave his kokum one last look filled with longing, with worry. He shook himself and marched across the clearing.

Jared jogged to keep up. When they reached the spring and its small pool, he collapsed onto some ferns. His bones sagged like cooked spaghetti. His muscles melted. Sauce on the pasta. He couldn't have moved if he saw a jet ready to crash down on top of him.

How was the pilot? He must've been rescued by now. He had to be okay. His flying had saved Jared. That kind of heroism shouldn't be rewarded with death. And if they saved Kyle's family from the monster? Well, then they should be rewarded with *their* lives.

Hah. Some part deep inside had known they were dead—*walking dead*—as soon as he'd accepted that this nightmare was real. He wasn't sure why he'd avoided the truth of it for so long. But now he was glad he had, or he might have really given up sooner. Now there was a reason to keep going. They had to keep *Wîhtiko* from escaping into that other world, their world.

"Thought you'd be snoring by now." Kyle's voice barely registered above the buzz of Jared's thoughts.

"Stupid hamster brain is on the run." Jared realized he was staring at the leaves overhead but not seeing them. He draped one arm over his eyes.

"Yeah. Mine, too. We had a hamster when Dad was still alive. Cat ate it."

"Seriously?"

"Um-hmm. Little brother, Sam, was three. He wanted to play with it on the floor. Ten seconds after he got it out of the cage, the cat pounced from behind the couch."

"Nasty."

"Yeah. So Sam's screaming, the cat's chowing down, and Dad storms in and blames me." Kyle snorted. "Maybe because I was rolling on the floor laughing."

"Hadn't you fed the cat? If it wasn't hungry it'd probably just play with the hamster."

"Maybe. But the cat's job was catching mice. Usually it had to go outside and hunt."

"You didn't feed your cat?"

"We did that day. That's why I was laughing. I tried to tell Dad. It was like we'd set up a fast food restaurant for the cat. Fast food pounce-thru. Dad didn't think it was funny. Sent me to Kokum's next door so he could calm Sam down."

"If that'd been me, my dad would've slapped me," Jared said. "He was the flyswatter and I was the fly. All he ever did was swat; that's the excuse Mom used to divorce him. Funny, he hasn't touched me since. And Mom was remarried a month after the divorce was final. She's never admitted it, but I think old step-dad was in the picture before the split."

"Tough break."

"Not as tough as yours. My dad didn't die. He's still around in body. When he can't avoid me. Did your mom leave your dad? Is that what you meant when you said she was gone?"

The breeze sifted leaves. Jared was trying to convince his arm to lift so he could turn and look at Kyle when he finally said, "No."

After another pause Kyle added, "And yes. Mom, she took off right after my brother was born. Headed west. First we heard she was seen on the way to Prince George. Then we heard she'd maybe been spotted on the streets in Vancouver. Then nothing."

Missing. Just like they were. Maybe she ended up in this spirit world, lost forever. Wooziness washed over Jared. He was sinking. Under the leaves. Into the cool black dirt. Roots wrapping around him. Round and round. To where? A memory floated by, of his mom playing with him, laughing as she tugged his toes. This little piggie went to market? Should have stayed home. This little piggie had roast beef. This little piggie had none. Roast beef would taste *sooo* good right now. Stomach too tired to growl. Too. Freaking. Tired.

- ⸻ -

Jared woke up wondering why pigs would eat roast beef.

His stomach squeezed and he curled up, as if protecting it. Another constriction moved lower, into his bowels. His eyes flew open and he groaned. Darkness enveloped him, thick and tinted with smoke.

"Kyle," he whispered. "Kyle?"

A grunt.

"Wake up. I have to take a dump." A vise gripped his gut. Another groan, this one edged with pain. "Now, Kyle. Like, right now."

"So go," came the mumbled reply.

"It's dark." Jared cupped his stomach as more pain rippled deep inside. "Got toilet paper?"

"No. Use moss."

"Pitch black out. Give me your flashlight."

Now Kyle sounded wide awake. "Are you crazy? That's a signal flare out here. Just feel your way a dozen steps or so behind us." Jared heard him rustling around. Then, "Here. Moss. There's a whole bed of it around this side of the spring."

Something bumped Jared's back, then shoulder. He took the handful of moss from Kyle's fist. Then the vise tightened again and he scrambled up and ran with branches smacking him. Stumbled. Pushed past a few more trees. Kicked a rotten log and stepped over. Fumbled with the buttons on his jeans. He crouched, half leaning on the log. His bowels emptied with a gush. The smell slammed into him and he bent sideways over the log, gagging, choking. Then vomiting. What little was in his stomach all ended up on the forest floor.

He held the moss to his face to block the stench. Waited. After a few minutes, he decided his pipes were clean and he used the moss. Moved quickly away from the stinking pile. A spruce bough brushed his shoulder, as if tapping him to ask him what he wanted.

A proper bathroom. A shower. Toothpaste. Clean clothes.

Home.

Even his parents. Even if it seemed they didn't want him. Well, right now he wanted them. More than anything. He always shrugged off hugs, but oh, the comfort of arms wrapping around you. Keeping you safe. The spruce bough patted him.

Sighing, Jared eyed the darkness. There were, apparently, various shades of black, if you stopped long enough to look at them. Silhouettes towered around him, and stars sprinkled the sky where he could see it, but their light remained as far from him as home. He realized with a jolt that he had no idea where the spring was. What direction had he run? The only thing he knew was where the hill lay, blacker than black, like a cosmic whirlpool pulling even shadows into its maw. Its tide sucking them to its center.

His stomach squeezed again, not with another round of the runs but with an all-too-familiar dread. He was alone. Alone in the dark with nasty things that could see when he was nearly blind.

Did bears hunt at night? Or cougars? He'd read somewhere that cougars lay in wait for their prey, jumped them from behind. He spun around, heart thudding. Searched the night for the glint of eyes. Or would a claw-tipped body tackle him without warning?

Panic began to scratch his throat. Very quietly, he whispered, "Kyle?" Then a bit louder. Louder. Then regular talking to a store clerk volume. Joshing with friends volume.

Finally, a reply. His name returned. Relief relaxed his muscles. Nothing had been drawn by his voice. He was still standing, still able to move.

"I'm lost," he called, taking a tentative step in the direction of the voice.

The night breeze carried his name from a different direction. He hesitated. Which one was Kyle? Chill shivered over him. His breathing rasped. What had Kyle said? His name rustled the leaves again, the tone filled with...worry? Was it Dad? Heart drumming, he slid his foot in that direction. Grasses rattled. He froze, pulse crashing like cymbal strikes.

Kyle had said to not go searching if the wind called his name. Which voice was the wind?

"Jared?"

He jerked his head toward the sound. Then back when the other voice called. They were too similar. How could he tell?

"*Moniyaw?* What the hell are you doing? Get back here."

Jared released his breath and smiled to himself. *That* was Kyle. He headed toward the sound. A frustrated sigh seemed to whisper behind him.

About every five seconds Kyle said, "This way."

The trip back to the spring was much slower than leaving had been.

When Jared reached the spring and sank onto a bed of moss, Kyle said, "You crashed into the bush like a madman.

You were supposed to stay close. What was that about?"

Jared lay back on the moss and let the stars above the clearing fill his vision. He squinted so they became a pleasant blur. His stomach seemed limp and rubbery, like a balloon that had lost its air. His legs felt the same. He was safe here. The voice had stopped calling as soon as he turned away from it. Should he tell Kyle? His gut flopped over. He rested one hand on his midsection. "I will never eat another rose hip. Ever."

"The runs?"

Jared groaned in reply.

"Should've let you take the flashlight with all that yelling you did. Damage is done now."

Damage done. Jared whispered, "I heard another voice out there."

Kyle's breathing huffed loudly, then eased. "How did you know which voice to follow?"

"It only called Jared. You called me *Moniyaw*."

A grunt. "Might as well sleep. Dawn's coming soon."

If it had followed him, they'd hear it thundering toward camp, wouldn't they? Jared decided to believe it because he really wanted more sleep. The emergency pit stop had wrung him out. "Kyle?"

"Mmm?"

"Remember the cat, how you laughed about serving it fast food pounce-thru when it usually hunted outside?" Exhaustion was sneaking up on him again. He felt himself starting to slide into sleep and he fought to stay awake for a few more minutes.

"What about it?"

Jared's voice slurred as he worked to get the idea out. "Maybe trying to feed *Wîhtiko* was the right idea. But maybe we can just use food to lure it...somewhere. Trap it."

Between one breath and the next, sleep ambushed him.

- ——— -

The dawn was heralded by ravens *qworking* in the tree-tops. They woke Jared, but didn't terrify him the way the owl's screech had that first night. He was pretty sure an owl wouldn't frighten him now either. There were far more terrifying things in this forest.

Jared curled into a tighter ball. The deerskin shirt kept a lot of the cold at bay, but a chill crawled over his body like a million ants. His exhaustion must have been deeper than he'd imagined for him to not notice the cold. He rolled over and saw that Kyle was gone.

Jared bolted to his feet. Pivoted, cold forgotten. He was about to call out when he spotted Kyle's backpack and rifle propped against a tree. His breath whooshed out. Kyle chose that second to return. He must have seen Jared's worried frown because he cocked one eyebrow. "Miss me?"

"Shut up." Jared settled back on the moss and stared at the rifle. Roast beef. Roast anything would taste so good right now. "What's for breakfast?"

"Got a couple rose hips in my pocket." Kyle produced them and held out his hand.

Edible, huh? Red globes of bowel-melting torture. Jared's stomach twisted. "Asshole."

"Interesting choice of words." Without lifting his gaze, Jared knew Kyle was grinning.

"It's not freaking funny. You must have guts of iron."

"They ran through me, too. I was just...quieter about it." Kyle tossed the remaining rose hips into the forest. He filled the canteen from the spring and gave it to Jared.

After quenching his thirst, Jared returned the canteen and wiped his mouth. "We can't live on just water. Even a pathetic city boy like me knows that."

Kyle drained the flask, refilled it, and attached it to its ring on the backpack. His expression got solemn. "We'll figure something out. I caught a fish once. I can do it again."

"But we don't have time for things like fishing. We're lucky *Wîhtiko* didn't catch up with us while we were sleeping. It was close—close enough to call me." A huge shiver rippled across Jared's shoulders. Someone walking on his grave, his grandmother would've said.

"Yeah. Us, we owe *Wesakechak* a huge debt for leading *Wîhtiko* away again, I'm thinking. Maybe even last night. Maybe that's why it didn't keep calling. But you're right about no time. We'll have to keep eating whatever the forest offers."

Jared grimaced at the thought as he swept his fingers through the spring's pool. So hungry. No fish here, though. No frogs. Not even a mouse peeking out from under a nearby plant. Thinking of eating mice? *Sick.* Insanity, all of it, especially what he'd considered last night, which of course Kyle had to bring up.

"So?" Kyle leaned against the backpack. "Last night. What was that stuff about trapping *Wîhtiko*?"

Jared thought of that flat expanse of rock on the hilltop. A table. *Wîhtiko's* table. He winced as a picture started to form—of him on that rock, frozen by a scream, of *Wîhtiko* lurching toward him. He shook his head violently. "This is *so* screwed up. I feel like we need to go up the hill, maybe find some way to trap it up there? There's something up there...something I can't..." He smacked the side of his head, willing himself to remember. Failing. "I can't quite remember, but I will when I see it."

"So let's go."

"Just like that?"

"Kokum's time is running out. If *Wîhtiko* gets to her, to Moshum, or...to Sam..."

With a nod, Jared rose and motioned for Kyle to lead the way.

- ——— -

The dread started in halfway up the hill, at a low boil again deep in his gut. But no adrenaline rush accompanied the bubbling unease. They had climbed as fast as possible and Jared was winded. Starving. He almost told Kyle to leave him, not that Kyle would. He'd be more likely to carry him up in a fireman's lift. The thought of being left alone, halfway up the hill that had plunged them into this nightmare, twisted his stomach into an even bigger knot and gave him the strength to take another step. Then another.

They were both heaving air. Kyle found two pieces of deadfall that worked as walking sticks, and they hiked upward in slow motion. Jared's length of branch was forked at one end so he used it like a crutch, leaning on it with each step.

When they finally reached the crest, Jared expected the sun to be setting, like it had been the first time they'd climbed the hill, but it was still rising toward midday. Exhaustion and the long climb had only made it feel like they'd hiked all day. The blue sky was whitewashed with a gauzy curtain of smoke, its sweet smell at odds with the stinging in Jared's eyes and nose. He collapsed beside the hill's cap of flat stone. When Kyle said he was going to see if he could spot the swamp where the plane had crashed, Jared waved him away. Minutes later he was back. Jared raised his eyebrows and Kyle shook his head.

Of course the jet wasn't visible. Nothing else had gone right these last few days; why should that be any different? Jared rested against an outcropping, took a drink from the offered canteen, and closed his eyes when he handed it back.

Had he ever been this tired? So bone weary that even lifting a canteen was an effort that left him shaking. It was the lack of food, he knew, but knowing didn't help.

Jared felt himself drifting, knew he shouldn't sleep because he wouldn't wake up, not until *Wîhtiko* was ripping his arm off to gnaw on it like a drumstick. He forced the words out. "Do you think they'll ever find us? Our bodies, I mean."

"If that's all you've got to say you can shut the hell up." The vehemence of Kyle's words jolted through Jared. He opened his eyes to see Kyle leaning against a boulder with his long legs stretched out in front of him. Kyle's gaze brimmed with anger and fear. Mostly anger. He spat onto the ground. "You said you'd help save my family."

"How? I can barely move."

Kyle's only answer was a stare, one so full of disappointment that Jared cringed. He had promised; he had said he was part of Kyle's tribe. Was his word worth so little? They hadn't seen *Wesakechak* since the swamp, not in human or wolverine form. There was no one else to help Kyle. He'd never had anyone depend on him for anything before, except maybe for access to his parents' cash. That couldn't be compared to saving someone's life. He recalled treading water in the lake and resuscitating Kyle, actually rescuing him when it had always been the other way around. Being useful. Having a purpose. It had felt good. For that one moment, he had mattered. To Kyle, at least.

"Okay," Jared said. "I'll try. Any ideas?"

"You were the one who talked about traps."

Silence smothered them, spread out to cloak the hill. Only the wind shuffled through the nearby trees, carrying the intensifying smell of smoke. Jared licked his lips, thought he could taste the smoke. "The fire's getting closer, isn't it?"

"Yeah."

We're going to be charbroiled. Jared didn't say it out loud. "Any chance *Wîhtiko* could be burned?"

Kyle sat up. He frowned at Jared. Or in his direction. It seemed as if he was looking through Jared. "A heart of ice. I suddenly have this memory of someone, my dad maybe, telling me *Wîhtiko* has a heart of ice. How could I forget that?"

"Ice?" Jared tried to fathom the logistics of an ice heart keeping something alive, but couldn't. The how didn't matter now anyway. "So fire might be something it's afraid of."

"Maybe."

They lapsed into silence again. Jared tried to imagine a scenario where *Wîhtiko* ended up barbequed but they escaped. If it came to that, he thought idly, it would be better to go up in flames with the monster than let it destroy more lives. Odd that the thought didn't bother him. More proof of his exhaustion.

"You know..." Jared stared at the sky. "None of this has improved my view of the Great Outdoors."

A laugh burst from Kyle. "Being thrown into the spirit world isn't my usual outdoor experience."

"And being chased by supernatural monsters?"

"First time, I swear."

"Then how did your kokum know about it? Know it was dangerous to go up the hill, I mean. And know when we were near her?" Jared raised his hand. "Wait. You said your... not Kokum..."

"Moshum."

"Right. That he had told you a story about it happening before. So what happened?"

"Don't ask."

"I just did."

"The ancestor was lost, I think is what Moshum said. They only knew his fate because of Kokum's Dene grandfather, who was a dreamer like Kokum. She talks about having a 'strange feeling in the breast.' How dreamers describe premonitions, I guess."

"So a dreamer is a witch doctor?"

"No. A shaman maybe. Dreamers get visions, of people, of animals, or animal spirits. But this grandfather dreamed about the lost ancestor, who came to him and warned him about the hill. Maybe Kokum received a vision from a spirit when we went up the hill, or a warning from that same ancestor. I don't know. But after that, the fire and sweetgrass and her prayers combined, I think."

"I've never been into church or anything, but I like the idea that she's praying for us."

"Yeah."

"You're lucky, having someone who cares that much. I'm trying to imagine either of my parents praying. Not happening, dude. They...aren't really into parenting."

"They just give you money instead?"

"Pretty much."

Kyle snorted. "Don't expect me to feel sorry for you."

Still staring blankly at the sky, Jared smiled sadly. "Money buys a lot of junk, Kyle, but it doesn't buy a praying kokum. Or a way out of this nightmare."

Was there a way out? There had to be. Jared tried to think. He rubbed his sore eyes. Cursed his tiredness. A gust of wind plundered through the treetops on the far side of the rock tabletop—he heard it approaching. It careened around the rocks and buffeted against them, carrying a stench stronger than the smoke.

"Wind's shifting," Kyle said, as if Jared hadn't noticed. "Could be bad news. We'd better look."

Jared struggled to his feet and leaned on his makeshift crutch. "What's that stink? It's not fire." Why did that seem familiar? Another gust of wind pushed smoke into his face and wiped out every other smell. He rubbed his eyes.

Kyle rose more slowly. He left his pack and rifle by the rock and climbed onto the flat expanse of stone. Jared followed. It would make a great landing pad for a rescue helicopter, he thought, and immediately hoped it never happened. He wouldn't wish this horror show on anyone else.

Smoke hung thick over the northern landscape and drifted east mostly, a gray veil over the green valley. Though Kyle was right that it was shifting toward them. On the downslope of the next hill, the occasional flame flared bright enough to be seen through the smoke. As they watched, the wind pushed one arm of flames south along the western slope below them. It was an octopus, fiery tentacles stretching out to surround the hill.

"There's nowhere to run now, is there?"

"It's still clear to the southeast."

"But that's the direction we came from. That's where *Wîhtiko* is."

"Then this is where we make our stand. As Crazy Horse said: *Hóka-héy*, today is a good day to die."

"What does *hóka-héy* mean?"

"It's Lakota. It means 'Let's do this.'"

"I've heard of Crazy Horse. There's this insanely big monument people are carving into a mountain in the Black Hills, in South Dakota, not far from that one with the American presidents' faces."

"Rushmore," Kyle said. "I've seen pictures. Me, I'd love to go there, to see the Crazy Horse memorial."

"We should go together."

Kyle peered at Jared, as if unsure of his sincerity. What he saw must have reassured him because a smile lifted one side of his mouth. "Sure."

Warmth lifted Jared's spirits for a moment, as if that one word carried enough hope to actually get them home. If he did get home, Jared knew the pressure would be to walk away, to say thanks and leave Kyle in his small house where he shared a bedroom with his little brother. To forget this. To forget Kyle's part in it. To forget the Cree guy who had rescued him. Maybe his parents would throw some money at Kyle in conspicuous gratitude—even though money couldn't begin to pay the deep debt Jared owed Kyle. But allow Jared to associate with him in any way? Not likely.

Reason # whatever—I've lost count—that we couldn't be friends: my parents wouldn't allow it.

Still, that one word—*sure*—promised more than rescue. It whispered of friendship. *Maybe...*

Wordlessly they drifted to the southeast side of the table-top rock and scanned the green valley with a haze hanging over it. No movement indicated *Wîhtiko's* whereabouts.

Jared sniffed. "There's that stink again. I caught a whiff of it a few minutes ago." He reached for a memory from the beginning of this ordeal, and it felt like he was delving years into the past. Decades. "That first day. Remember?

We smelled it then, too."

"Yeah. A cave."

Right. A cave. Jared's memory lurched. "A weird noise came out of that cave." Jared licked his lips again, accepted the canteen from Kyle. After sipping some water, he continued, "Maybe that cave is *Wihtiko's* lair. The opening was small, but it might have come out of there. It was smaller before we fed it."

Jared trailed after Kyle and his thoughtful frown to the cluster of small and mid-sized boulders where they'd found the cave entrance. Jared clapped one hand over his mouth and nose to filter the vile stench and squinted into the narrow tunnel. Kyle crouched beside him and pointed into the darkness. "There's a light source. That might mean ..."

"Another entrance on the other side of the hill?"

"I think so. I bet you're right, Jared. This is *Wihtiko's* lair."

23

Plans

The northeast face of the rock shelf was a tumble of boulders that spilled down a steep slope, almost a cliff, for three meters before easing into a gentler, tree-covered decline. Roughly two meters down the bluff, a visible trail snaked between rocks of all sizes and disappeared around a jut of the stone bulwark.

When they reached the trailhead, they both scanned the area, searching for any sign that *Wîhtiko* might be in the area, but the forest was eerily quiet. Apprehension beaded sweat along Jared's hairline. Shredded fingers of smoke floated over the treetops, thinning as they stretched away from the flames on the next hill. A blast of wind, thick with the sweet burning smell of wood and leaves, hit them in the face. A distant tree exploded into flame and burned like a thin candle, fire shooting skyward.

Jared coughed and waved the air by his nose, trying to inhale something fresh. He stifled another cough. "What do we do if *Wîhtiko* is inside?" He swallowed, mouth dry.

Kyle shrugged. "Race to the fire. Hope we're fast enough." Worry fanned out from his eyes. He glanced over his shoulder and motioned for Jared to lead.

They picked their way along the rocky trail, short cliff rising on their left. When they reached the bulwark, Jared rested his hand on the nearly squared-off stone, cool and smooth. The monster's castle. Once again, he felt as if he were in a movie. Why did the people in horror flicks always do such stupid things, like going into basements after they'd heard noises, or entering spooky houses? At least he had a reason for this stupidity. Sort of.

Kyle whispered, "Want me to go first?"

"No." *Yes, yes, yes.* "Just stay close." Jared's dry mouth became drier still.

He curled his fingers over the corner of rock and peered around it. Though he'd expected it, he still recoiled at the sight of the entrance.

"Is it there?" Kyle whispered.

Jared nodded, eyes wide, heart galloping. The opening was half blocked by a boulder, but was easily big enough for Kyle to enter. The smoke couldn't mask the awful reek. Jared edged around the corner of rock, stuck close to the wall and sidled toward the yawning entrance. It looked more mouth-like with every step. He hunkered down by the boulder. Kyle bumped his elbow as he settled beside him. He flinched.

They couldn't see the trail behind them, and couldn't see in without exposing themselves. Jared's pulse ratcheted up. The stench roiled out of the cave and he almost gagged, then held his forearm over his nose and mouth so he mostly smelled deerskin. Kyle copied him.

Before they'd come searching for the cave, Kyle had retrieved his flashlight from his backpack. Now he pulled it from his breast pocket and gave Jared a questioning look. Jared nodded. His stomach lurched at his counterfeit bravery.

From behind the boulder, Kyle shone the light into the cave, slicing through the darkness in narrow cuts. When nothing emerged, they approached the black mouth. Kyle's light searched inside, flicked over litter, bits of bone, strips of deerskin. It paused on a skull that looked distinctly human, jumped away. Hungry as he was, Jared was relieved there was nothing in his stomach to spew.

Light spilled into the space from an opening high in the far wall and was swallowed whole by the cave's oppressive dark. The flashlight's beam skittered around it. The smaller crevice, which had to be the first one they'd found, was an attic window, but a window at the end of a skinny tunnel. Kyle skimmed the flashlight beam up and down the wall, pausing on the lumps and bumps between the floor and window. Jared wondered what he was looking for.

He couldn't stand the foulness any longer. The deerskin sleeve had ceased to be effective; the stink permeated everything. He retreated to the boulder outside and watched another tree combust on the valley floor, this one much closer. The fire's crackle reached him as faint static. Kyle joined him a minute later.

Jared hunched his shoulders. "So? Could we lure *Wihtiko* back into the cave?"

"If we do, will it send us back into our own world?"

Jared considered that. "It's our only play. How do we trick it into going back in?" He tried to picture it. Why would *Wihtiko* enter the cave unless it was chasing one of them? Jared recalled the way Kyle had examined the wall under the window so closely. "You already saw it. One of us has to lead *Wihtiko* in there, then get out through the window." And then it hit him. His stomach turned as hard as the boulder he sat on. "You wouldn't fit through that smaller tunnel."

Kyle winced, expression furrowed with guilt.

"I have to be the bait." Jared said it aloud to convince himself of the statement's truth. He didn't need a comment and Kyle didn't offer one. Jared returned to the cave's beckoning gorge and stared at its cyclops eye of light. He shuddered. "Live bait."

— ——— -

"There's one thing wrong with this plan," Jared said, "other than the fact that I might get freaking eaten."

"You won't get eaten. A person moves faster scared than anything does angry. Or, well, hungry." Kyle shrugged, almost hopefully. "Your idea to block the main entrance is good."

They both peered up at the pile of rocks placed above the mouth of the cave, waiting to become a Kyle-induced avalanche. They'd dragged a dead tree to their stone heap and had positioned it as a lever. Who knew that physics would turn out to be so useful?

Jared shook his head. "It might take too long to pry that big rock into falling. And if others need to be physically pushed, then *Wîhtiko* might have time to get out again... unless it's busy dismembering me." Memories of *Wîhtiko* rending apart that deer with the ease of tearing up a cardboard box caused him to shiver.

The smoke was giving Jared a headache, making his already fuzzy mind fuzzier. Kyle had said that *Wesakechak* had convinced an ermine to go down *Wîhtiko's* throat and destroy it from the inside out. Now Jared had his own interior ermine; he was convinced of it. Sometimes he thought he could actually hear it chewing. He definitely felt its sharp little teeth ripping his stomach open.

The smoke was slowly filling his lungs with foggy death. The line of advancing fire was constantly visible now, a red and orange assault on the valley floor. Its snapping had grown louder as the sound seemed to rise with the smoke. Soon it would gain a beachhead on the hill itself and begin the climb. One spot flared yellow as it consumed something especially dry. Flames leaped into the next tree.

Flames. Jared sat up straighter on his rock. "We'll trap it inside with fire."

"If we wait for the fire to get here to block the cave, we might not escape it."

"Right. But we could pile dry sticks and grass in the cave entrance, and more beside it that you can shove over after

Wîhtiko goes inside. Make our own fire."

"Before or after the rock slide?"

Jared glanced up. "Before. The fire might also distract it and give me another minute to escape." He sighed. "Which leads us to another problem."

"What? It sounds like everything's covered."

Jared huffed air in and out. In and out. Then he blurted, "You might've noticed I—I don't do so well when I'm..."

Kyle swept his hand, palm up, indicating Jared should continue.

"I don't handle being alone very well."

"Understatement. But if it helps, you won't actually be in the cave alone."

"You think it's helpful to tell me I won't be alone because a freaking monster will be chasing me up the wall hoping to snack on me?" Not even a meal. Just a snack.

Wîhtiko-snack.

Jared groaned, doubled over, forehead against knees, and clasped his hands over the back of his head. He drew air that didn't reach his lungs. Shallow puffs. *Breathe,* he told himself. *Breathe.* His voice was muffled against his thighs. "I'm not. Brave. Just. Afraid."

"That's total bull. You've kept up with me for days, Jared. You saved me in the lake. Bravery is acting even when you're afraid." Kyle nudged him. "Sometimes afraid is the smartest thing you can be."

Jared gave a jerky nod. He wished he didn't feel quite so smart. He finally managed to inhale deeply enough that his lungs stopped aching.

"Okay. Let's get that bonfire ready." Kyle's voice anchored Jared. He straightened. Nodded again, firmer this time. Help build the fire; that's all he had to do right now. Focus on that. Only that.

They scrambled into the forest, gathered as much kindling as they could plus a few larger pieces of deadfall. Exhaustion dogged Jared's heels, but the possibility that this all might actually end—and soon—oozed some energy into his muscles. They each scavenged an armful of dry grass and heaped it with the twigs and branches into two piles, a smaller one in the cave entry and a larger one beside it ready to be pushed onto the smaller one after *Wîhtiko* passed.

Sitting back to back on a large rock, they rested and drank the last of the water.

"If I could have a last meal," Jared said, "it would be an extra-large pizza. Double cheese, piled so thick with meat that the slices look like deli sandwiches without a top piece of bread."

"Yeah. With lots of mushrooms."

"No anchovies."

"Hell, no. Or onions."

"Red peppers would be okay."

"Maybe triple cheese. One layer on the sauce, under the meat."

Jared moaned his appreciation. His stomach squeezed painfully, anticipating the first bite of that mirage pizza. He could almost smell it. But no, the only real smells here were smoke and cave stink. He pushed to his feet and peered north, eyes burning. The fire continued to creep up the hill, sending smoke ahead of it like some kind of trail scout, thickening the air and making it increasingly hard to breathe. The sound was constant now. More than crackling, the fire hissed and spat. A deadly, snaking hydra slithering up the hill.

"Ready?" Kyle asked. He handed Jared the small flashlight and double-checked that his lighter was working. He had returned from one scavenging trip with his rifle, and now he loaded a single bullet into the chamber and pushed the bolt forward.

Jared bit his lip. Don't think, he told himself. Just act. One step, then another. Blank mind. *It's not working.* "I'll never be ready. Just do it."

Kyle nodded. "Whatever happens, I'm glad you're part of my spirit world tribe."

Jared wanted to say, *Same here,* but he couldn't make his smoke-filled, desert mouth work. He gave Kyle a weak smile and a weak punch on his arm.

Kyle stood beside Jared and aimed the rifle above the fire. For a long moment he only squinted down the barrel, squinted and tapped the wooden stock, a deep scowl furrowing his brow.

The single shot rang loud and clear.

24

Flames

Jared stood beside the corner jut of rock where he could see both the forest and the cave entrance. His legs jittered. He wanted to retreat to the cave right now, but *Wihtiko* had to see him, had to see where he was going. This was crazy. So freaking crazy. He'd been able to mostly ignore the panic, but now its low boil was starting to bubble higher, stirring up a decidedly sick feeling deep in his gut.

He glanced to where Kyle was waiting behind a cluster of rocks beyond the cave. If he couldn't block off the entrance this was all for nothing. Realization ambushed him. What if *Wihtiko* screamed? That awful, blood-freezing scream erupting from its tattered mouth. Fear shivered over Jared's limbs as he remembered the feeling of being encased in ice, unable to move. His breath huffed out. If that happened, Kyle would be frozen outside the cave; he'd be frozen inside it.

Panic seethed up toward the rim of sanity. Jared slapped at his shirt, needing something to stuff in his ears. Patted his jeans. Stopped over the right pocket. He pulled out his iPod, stared at it blankly. He'd forgotten he had it, was so used to it being in his pocket that he never felt it anymore. His jeans seemed to have shrunk against his skin and he fumbled to slide his hand deeper into the pocket. The cord teased his fingertips. He stretched his fingers, pinched the cord. Tugged.

One earbud popped out of the pocket. The other was caught. He frantically pulled the whole pocket inside out, found the other earbud snagged in a hole. Worked it free with shaking fingers.

He waved the earbuds in the air. "Kyle! Plug your ears!" He stuffed the buds into his own ears, sighed with relief, and tucked the dangling cord inside his shirt. He began scanning the edge of the forest. How far away was it? How fast could it travel? Overhead, ravens flapped away from the fire. He squinted at them, wishing he and Kyle could escape so easily.

Something burst from the trees. He fell back two steps before he realized it was a pair of deer. He braced a hand against the rock, trying to get his rampaging fear under wraps. The deer bounded across the clearing, also away from the fire. They disappeared in a flash of white tails.

He had barely calmed himself when his name whispered through his mind. But he was wearing his earbuds! *Jared…* *Jared.* His foot started sliding forward, a puppet foot tugged by a string. "No!" His yell was muffled. "No freaking way, *Wîhtiko*!"

The taste of smoke coated Jared's mouth and scratched his throat. What if *Wîhtiko* wanted to let the fire eat them?

Maybe it liked barbeque. *Shut up, moron.* Maybe it was still hours away and had just called his name to torment him. Had it even heard the shot?

Then he saw...movement, near where the deer had disappeared. No animal would be moving closer to the fire. *No, please, no. I'm not ready. I need more time.*

For a second, maybe a lifetime, he could only stare. A gray shadow zigzagged through the trees. Closer. Closer. It was here. *Oh shit. Don't think. Act. Walk through the fear. Screw that. Run. Run through the fear.* He took a step. Jerked to a standstill. *Remember Kyle's family.* He faced the forest and yelled, "This way! This way!"

The shadow veered in Jared's direction.

His gut dropped over a cliff. He spun and raced along the track, catching a glimpse of Kyle ducking behind rocks. A step into the cave the stench hit him with the force of a train t-boning a car. Smacked his lungs flat. He stumbled. Pulled the flashlight from his back pocket. Switched it on. The beam winked around the room. Ceiling, floor, wall. Blink. Blink. Blink. It quavered as he stepped forward, toward the light filtering in through the attic-window exit. It was farther away than he expected. He bolted forward.

A rock caught his toe. He sprawled onto the floor. The flashlight skittered away and snuffed out. Darkness and rasped breathing and stink choking him. Small circle of light ahead; larger half moon of light behind.

Jared retched. Pressed his hand on the floor to push up. Fingers brushed bone. Horror crashed through him. He scrambled up, stumbled toward his escape. Fell again. His cheek smacked the dirt. He gaped at a sliver of light falling across a skull, eye sockets staring hollowly at him. He yelled. Leapt up. Kept yelling though it sounded distant.

Swearing, cursing, calling *Wîhtiko* every foul name he'd ever heard anywhere. He backed away from the skull, spun, and charged the wall. Dread foamed into anger. That he was here, that any of this was happening. Vitriol spilled from his mouth, though he hardly heard it through the earplugs. He kept swearing as he smacked the wall, fingers strained toward the window, so close but out of reach.

He glanced behind. The half-moon of light from the doorway was distorted. By *Wîhtiko*. Jared screamed his fear and hatred, screamed and climbed, scurried up the wall like a spider. Fingers curled over the ledge of the window. He found a crack, wedged his fingers in. Pulled. Treaded air with his legs. Found purchase and pushed. Elbows on the ledge now, he wriggled and wormed his way forward.

Glanced back to see a form silhouetted by fire. Kyle's bonfire. Jared kept yelling. "Freaking asshole! You're not going to get me. You're not! You're not!"

He writhed and twisted. Forward. Forward. The tunnel stretched. Too far. Too freaking far. The ceiling brushed his head. He ducked. Wiggled.

Something grabbed his ankle. His mind flashed a picture of bleeding stumps hooked onto his foot. His yells melted into terror. He kicked. Pulled with his hands. Kicked and kicked at the lumpy grip.

Rumbling, thumping, thudding. He felt the rocks falling more than heard them. Jared scraped forward, felt himself being dragged back. He held to a crack in the rock. The edge dug into his hands as he was stretched. Pulled thin.

The muted scream slammed into him with the force of an avalanche. The sound packed around him, into his eyes, into his nose, down his throat. His fingers froze into claws. *No, no, no!* In his chest, he felt a kernel of warmth. He focused on it as *Wîhtiko* began dragging him backward. He wrapped that seed in anger. Hot, gurgling anger. Like boiling water melting ice cubes, he pushed the cold away. Instead of swearing, he prayed as he flailed for another handhold. *Help me, help me. Whoever you are. Help. Me.* He found a knob of rock and wrenched himself forward a few inches.

The light ahead switched off. *I'm dying. I'm being torn apart. Not like this. Not—*

Fingers grasped his wrist. Kyle. Jammed into the tunnel. Blocking the light.

Hope surged. Jared's free foot became a jackhammer. Kick, kick, kick.

The captured foot snapped. Jared screamed. But it was free. Or his leg was. "Pull, Kyle! Pull!"

Kyle reeled him out of the hole and they both fell onto the grass and rocks below the tunnel mouth. Jared's stomach spasmed violently and for a minute he could only spit up stomach acid. He tugged the earbuds free and dropped them. Voice weak and shaky, he whispered, "My foot. Is it there? Did it pull off my foot?"

"Shoe's gone. Foot's there. It looks...twisted, broken maybe."

"Hurts. So freaking much."

"At least you're out. And *Wîhtiko* is inside. It's still bigger than me, so unless it can shrink really fast it might be trapped for now. The plan might've worked."

On the other side of the tabletop plateau, the fire crackled and howled above the wind. Jared scanned Kyle's worried face. "That's not the bonfire, is it?"

Kyle shook his head. "I'll carry you."

"What about your rifle and backpack?"

"Rifle's by the rock slide. Can't get to it. Nothing in the pack will help us now." He hesitated, ran to it, and came back with the forked walking stick. "Hang on to this. If I get too tired, at least you can hobble."

A howl of rage echoed down the tunnel, escaped. Sleet skated over Jared's skin. Kyle shuddered, too.

Kyle stuffed the stick down the back of Jared's deerskin shirt so the Y stuck out like some weird antenna. He helped Jared onto a boulder. Agony rocketed through his ankle and up his leg. As they were maneuvering to get Jared onto Kyle's back, Jared said, "It can't end with us going up in smoke." He wrapped his arms around Kyle's neck, and Kyle crooked his arms around Jared's thighs.

"Kokum's still praying." Kyle jostled him into a comfortable position.

Jared recalled that grain of warmth. "I think I felt her prayers in the cave."

Spots wavered across his vision. Everything started to swirl and fade. He bit his lip. Tasted blood. The woozy feeling retreated. From his perch he scanned the hillside. "The fire has cut off the swamp."

"Yeah. Me, I figure we should head to camp."

"To your kokum."

Kyle nodded. Started out at a brisk walk. Each step washed a fresh wave of pain up Jared's leg. But he held on, to Kyle and to consciousness.

They entered the trees. Smoke wafted around them like fog. Close by, fire cackled like something evil and alive.

And hungry.

25

Kokum

Jared drifted in and out of darkness. Coughed smoke out of his nose and lungs. Jolted back awake when Kyle stumbled only to fade again. He was bucked to consciousness when Kyle started to run.

The fire that now protected them from *Wîhtiko's* pursuit snapped and hissed behind them. A dragon come to life, devouring everything. Tongues of flame roared behind them.

Kyle raced downhill. Faster. Leaping, dodging. Branches slapped their heads, their arms and legs. Jared hung on as electric shocks of pain in his ankle flatlined into one buzzing, grinding, steady torment.

Trees blurred. The run edged into something wild and out of control. Kyle's fear telegraphed from his arms into Jared's legs as they squeezed. They fell. Bumped and rolled. Landed in a tangle, Kyle on top of Jared's legs. Jared on top of a rose bush.

He yowled in agony.

Kyle threw himself to the side and lay on the ground, gasping, chest heaving. Jared almost blacked out as he eased off the shrub. He pulled the walking stick out from the back of his shirt and propped himself up. Swearing quietly, he plucked a thorn from his neck. The deerskin shirt had saved him from any other barbs, but he could feel stinging on his back where the stick had scraped him. None of it compared to his throbbing ankle.

"I can't." Still sprawled on his stomach, Kyle gulped in air and coughed. "Nothing left. Sorry."

For now they seemed to have outpaced the fire. Thanks to Kyle. Jared plucked a rose hip. "Here. Maybe this will give you some energy."

Kyle turned his head but didn't lift it. A smile flicked over his lips and disappeared. "You eat it. I'd rather be roasted."

Jared couldn't return the smile. He struggled onto his good foot and propped the forked stick under his armpit. He extended his hand. "You wouldn't let me quit. I'm not letting you quit."

Kyle eyed the hand, then sighed and grabbed it. Once on his feet, he rested a hand on Jared's shoulder to steady himself. For a while, the path was wide enough to walk side by side, arms braced around each other. They fell into a lurching rhythm. Swing the stick forward, walk and hop, swing, walk and hop.

The path narrowed again. Kyle found another piece of deadfall he could turn into a cane and they both faltered and struggled forward. Gravity, more than anything, maintained their forward momentum.

Only Jared's skin stopped his pain and exhaustion from exploding into the air. He couldn't remember a time when he didn't hurt. It rubbed his bones, rippled along his muscles, pushed at his skin. Everything dimmed. Hearing, sight, smell, all fused into a haze. All that existed was the next step, the next micro burst of pain. Even that dulled with a weariness that went beyond anything he'd known. He couldn't have run, or even hobbled quickly—not to escape the fire, not to escape *Wîhtiko*. Not for anything.

Jared didn't notice gloom descending around him until Kyle's camouflaged back blended into the forest. His friend disappeared in growing darkness. "Kyle?" he whispered. No answer.

He shrugged, continued forward. A dozen steps later he glimpsed movement again. Followed it, knowing by the size it had to be Kyle. He wondered if he'd ever escape the smell of smoke or if it had seeped so deeply into his skin and hair that it would always be part of him. No city stink anymore, or ever again. Or maybe the smell of smoke was death catching up to him after all these days.

Something pricked his neck. An ember? He'd seen them floating in the smoke like fireflies. More pricks. He didn't try to brush them away. He didn't look back. He imagined that, in the dark, the advancing line of fire was clear, orange and red and dancing toward them, eating the forest, hungry for flesh. *Wîhtiko* in another form.

He wished he hadn't tossed that rose hip. His stomach had caved in. His own hunger was cavernous now, a presence as vivid as the pain in his ankle. Maybe *Wîhtiko* had left some of the deer carcass in the clearing. If only they could get there. He imagined himself falling on the dead animal, ripping into the raw meat with his teeth, blood dripping down his face and painting his hands. The possibility teased him forward.

When had it become dark? Jared peered ahead. The blackness was broken by a pale glow. Kyle's silhouette flickered in and out of the light. Fire. Had it surrounded them? Jared couldn't think, could only move forward. Fire. They could cook the remains of deer. Die with full stomachs.

Kyle shouted. Jared hobbled faster. He stopped five steps into a clearing. It seemed vaguely familiar. But different.

His gaze tracked Kyle, who had thrown aside his walking stick and was running toward a fire. Jared blinked to make sense of what he was seeing. Not a forest fire. A campfire. Then he noticed someone standing by the fire, arms spread wide.

Jared limped forward. Eyes burning, he watched as Kyle reached the figure. His kokum. He picked her up, swung her around. She was laughing. Jared bit his lip. Wished.

He startled as strong arms lifted him and cradled him like a baby. His crutch fell in the grass. For a second his body was tense—*Wîhtiko* had caught him! But he looked up, into a face lined and smiling in the campfire light. This had to be Kyle's grandfather, his moshum.

Now forms beyond the firelight became visible. A trailer. A tent. A big pickup truck that glinted red where light flickered over it.

Kyle's moshum set him gently down beside the fire but continued to hold him upright. Sudden fear choked Jared's throat. "The doorway has opened? *Wîhtiko*. The forest fire. We have to get away."

"No," a soothing voice said from beside him. He shifted to see Kyle and his kokum with arms around each other's waists. Kokum said, "You've closed the way. Whatever the two of you did in the spirit world sent you back to us."

"Back?" Emotion squeezed Jared's chest. "Really back?"

She nodded and held out her free arm. Jared stared at the comfort she offered, wanted so badly to go but something held him back. In that other place, he and Kyle had been tribesmen. But here, he was once again a stupid rich kid from the city. He had no right to force himself on them.

Kokum motioned with her fingers. "*Astam*. Come here." He bit his lip, still reluctant. She seemed to understand. "Kyle is *nôcicim*, my grandchild. He saved you, but you saved him, too, Jared. You are a grandchild of the heart."

Gulping back a clog of emotion, Jared hobbled into her embrace. Kyle thumped him on the back. He smiled against Kokum's camouflage jacket, so much like Kyle's. After a few minutes, they separated. Moshum settled Jared by the fire and went for a first aid kit. Kokum placed tin cups of warm liquid in their hands.

It smelled suspicious, but not nearly as bad as he did. Jared took a sip, scrunched his face. "What is this?"

"Willow bark tea. It will ease your pains." Kokum smiled, her face bronzed by the fire. She looked too young to be a grandmother.

Kyle focused on drinking his own tea with tiny sips. Jared slurped a bit, then looked to Kokum. "How did you know my name?"

"People are looking for you. I will have to phone the search and rescue team soon. But first, you need to drink, eat."

"How can you call anyone? There are no towers around here." That's what had gotten him into this mess. Something bit his neck. A mosquito, he realized. Out in the forest, it had been mosquitoes biting him, not forest fire embers.

"Sat phone." When Jared gave her a puzzled look, she clarified: "The search team left me a satellite phone. It's in my Big Red Stallion." She nodded toward the truck. "No towers needed."

Jared faced Kyle. "How are we going to explain being lost in the bush for four days?"

"It wasn't that long in this world," Kokum said. "Four days there, four days by the sweetgrass fire, but only one day in this world. The airplane crashed, oh, thirty hours ago, maybe. A helicopter took the pilot to Edmonton. He's alive, thanks to you two."

"Thanks to Kyle," Jared said. "I'm useless."

"Not completely," Kyle replied. "Only mostly."

They both laughed.

Moshum returned with the first aid kit and granola bars. Jared rolled his eyes and chewed slowly. Healthy had never tasted so good.

"Better than rose hips, huh?" Kyle smiled.

"That's for sure, along with pretty much every other food on the planet."

Kyle laughed. Relief energized them both. Their words stumbled over each other's to tell their story. Somewhere along the way, a small body emerged from the tent, curled up beside Kyle, and used his lap as a pillow.

They talked long into the night, the campfire warm and too inviting to leave. The company warmer. Kyle and Jared both opted to sleep by the fire.

Jared lay on his back and stared at the stars. Had it happened, really happened? His jacket was gone, replaced by a deerskin shirt. He had only one shoe. His ankle was braced and bandaged, pain dulled by willow bark tea and some red tablets. Badly sprained, Kyle's kokum said, not broken. Most importantly, not a *Wîhtiko* snack. Jared smiled.

The sky twinkled with dots of friendly light. No claustrophobic cave-like trailer for him, thanks. This was good. This kind of outdoor living he could almost come to enjoy. No mythical monsters chasing you, slavering over your flesh. *Enjoy that running shoe,* Wîhtiko. *I hope you choke on the gold stripes.*

Around the fire, they had all agreed that the boys could never tell the truth to the police, to any authorities, or even to Jared's parents. At best they would be accused of lying to get attention; at worst they would be locked in a psych ward and tested for days or weeks, until they recanted and said the truth was a lie.

No. *Wîhtiko* would walk through their nightmares, but that's where it would remain, except among those who knew better. And never, Jared decided, never would he walk anywhere Kyle's kokum warned him against.

Early the next morning, the camp burst to life as searchers descended upon it like a swarm of mosquitoes. Jared
picked out his dad in their midst, looking haggard. The
expression on his father's face spoke volumes: he was *not*
impressed by his son's disheveled hair, deerskin shirt and
borrowed boots. He frowned when he noticed the makeshift crutch.

He shouldered past everyone and clamped a hand on
Jared's shoulder. "You're safe."

"Hi, Dad." Jared couldn't think of anything to say. He
wished his dad would give him a hug, but he just stood, stiff
and awkward in his leather jacket and expensive shoes. Those
had to be the stupidest things to wear in the bush.

"What were you thinking, leaving the crash site? You
scared us half to death. Where were you?"

Scared *him* half to death? He had no idea. No freaking
idea. Jared shrugged and stepped back. "Dad. I want you to
meet someone." He waved Kyle over. "This is the guy who
kept this *Moniyaw* alive out in the bush. Kyle Badger, this
is my dad, John Frederickson."

Kyle looked distinctly uncomfortable. He scuffed at the
ground with his toe and muttered hello. He wouldn't meet
the gaze raking over him.

Jared's dad said, "You led my son into this god-forsaken
forest instead of waiting for rescue?" His expression twisted
into anger, and his fingers curled into fists.

"No, Dad," Jared interrupted. He hesitated, expecting a

verbal slap-down, then lifted his chin. If he could survive the last four days, he could make his father listen. "I panicked, got stupid, took off. Kyle saved me." He looked into Kyle's face. "He's my friend."

A smile crinkled out from Kyle's dark eyes. He gave a small nod. Jared's dad watched him like he was a rattlesnake about to strike.

Amazed that his father hadn't contradicted him, even though he looked suspicious, Jared felt bolstered, as if his father's silence were a lifejacket in choppy water. Maybe the fact that they'd had a rough time showed. Maybe, just maybe, his father was the tiniest bit impressed they had come through it. "And Dad, could you do something for us?" That shifted his attention away from Kyle. Some of the irritation eased, letting the lines fanning out from his eyes disappear. Jared licked his lips, then met his father's gaze to prove he meant business. "Could you arrange a trip to the Black Hills for me and Kyle?"

"What the hell for?" Surprise arched his eyebrows.

"To see the Crazy Horse monument." Jared grinned at his friend. "Private jet would be a great way to get there, I'm thinking." His father crossed his arms and gave Jared an assessing look, but didn't refuse. Jared knew then he'd probably get his request. *Who knows? Maybe Dad won't stop us from being friends after all. If Kyle can put up with me.* And even if his parents didn't like the idea of him being friends with Kyle, there were plenty of ways they could keep connected. He was old enough to choose his own friends. His dad's disapproval wasn't the least bit frightening compared to what they'd already been through.

Kyle snorted. "Aren't you afraid the plane will crash?"

"Not much chance it would happen twice, right?"

Kyle just rolled his eyes. They both laughed. A bird swooped overhead and seemed to join them, calling raucously. *Wha-ha-ha. Wha-ha-ha.* It landed on the rollbar of Kokum's Big Red Stallion. A Whiskey Jack.

Jared and Kyle simultaneously whispered, "*Wesakechak.*" They startled and looked at each other, then both waved at the bird in silent thanks.

The Whiskey Jack gave another chirping laugh and flew toward the hill, like a gray puff of smoke from a sweetgrass fire.

Author's Note

I'm grateful that Pajama Press continues to support my creative impulses, even when I venture into different genres. My appreciation goes to Gail Winskill and the whole team for believing in *The Hill* and for working their magic to turn it from a manuscript into a book. I also owe Gail thanks for the privilege of working with an editor of Linda Pruessen's caliber. Who else could help this revision-averse writer not mind the process at all? Thanks, Linda, for making revisions almost fun.

The seed for this story was planted when I heard that a friend was writing a story about a real plane crash, and my mind jumped to a "what if" scenario. As I read Cree legends and talked to people in the Cree community about *Wîhtiko,* my version of the legend became an amalgamation of those stories. I did not add anything to this story's *Wîhtiko* that

I didn't hear from at least one source.

Because Cree is originally an oral language, there are multiple spellings for several of the Cree words included in the story. My friend, Barb Belcourt, a member of Kelly Lake Community and a Cree teacher in our local school, went over my vocabulary list, and together we finalized the spelling of each word. I often opted for the simplest version. The one case where she convinced me to use a more complex spelling was with *Wihtiko* itself—this spelling seems to encapsulate the breathiness I heard when she pronounced the first syllable, and also acknowledges the fact that although there is a *g* sound in the word, no *g* exists per se in the Cree alphabet.

I also had some input on language issues from Jaret Cardinal, member of the Sucker Creek First Nation, and a few other people online. My thanks to everyone who assisted me as I strove to be faithful to the Cree language.

Barb and Jaret also read early versions of the manuscript and offered valuable comments on the story itself and on Cree culture and issues that pertained to the story. I wanted to be true to facets of modern Cree experiences through Kyle, my Cree teenager, but mostly I wanted him to be a well-rounded character readers could relate to. If I messed up, it was unintentional; it is also on me, because I had great feedback.

Kyle's surname came to mind because badgers are related to wolverines, and because, growing up in an area with both Cree and Métis, I remembered attending school with some Badgers. After I'd decided to use it, I checked the phone book for Wabasca, the real town my fictional character lives in. It turns out a lot of Badgers call Wabasca home, so I feel obligated to note that Kyle sprang completely from my imagination and isn't based on anyone I've ever met.

Before even my first readers and my publisher, my husband, Michael, is my primary support in every stage of creation and promotion, and I'm grateful. For this story in particular, I also need to thank the Canada Council and the Alberta Foundation for the Arts for support through the Alberta Creative Development Initiative (ACDI) program.

Thank you everyone. With your help, I enjoyed climbing this hill.